The real Brianne is the one before you. You should believe in her. Pete shook his head as if trying to dislodge the thought. Why was he going to so much trouble for one client? Sure she had great legs...and eyes that seemed to see all the way down to his soul. The way she looked at him as if she had known him for years. The more he was with her, the more he thought there had once been something between them.

The candle on the table flickered in the evening breeze, and for a moment Pete felt he was looking at a different woman. Black hair instead of ash blond, dark eyes instead of green. "Allie," he whispered, unthinking. As he lowered his head, he missed the slight tremble of her lips.

"Did you love her?" Brianne asked.

He was silent for a long time. "You know, we never had a chance to find out."

Brianne choked back the tears. *I have to tell him!* she screamed inside her head. *I have to tell him who I really am!*

And do you think he'll believe you?

Dear Reader,

When I sold my first two books in 1979, I felt proud to say I could never be considered a one-book author. Little did I know that fifty books later, I would still be doing what I love. How do I feel now, after I've written my fiftieth book? Tired. It has to do with feeling stunned that I've written so many books and haven't even considered stopping.

Ever since I can remember I've wanted to write books. My journalism adviser in college told me there was no future in writing fiction, but I knew it wasn't going to stop me. Through marriage, I took a bit of a detour, but writing was always in the back of my mind. I just needed that right story to start things off.

I've been very lucky to be in on the explosive growth of romance writing. To not only see what began back in the late seventies and how it evolved over the years but to be a part of it has been an experience not forgotten.

Everyone has been wonderful to stick with me each and every book. Hope you're all still with me when my hundredth book is published. I guess by then I really will be tired!

Linda Randall Wisdom

Linda Randall Wisdom

TWIST OF FATE

Harlequin Books

TORONTO • NEW YORK • LONDON
AMSTERDAM • PARIS • SYDNEY • HAMBURG
STOCKHOLM • ATHENS • TOKYO • MILAN
MADRID • WARSAW • BUDAPEST • AUCKLAND

There's a lot of people I'd like to thank for being there for me all these years, but I don't think I have enough room! So I'll thank the most important ones: My husband, Bob, for understanding when I drifted off into another world. My parents for not minding having an overimaginative daughter. My editors over the years who didn't flinch when I said "what if I did this?" My agent, Maureen Walters, who calls me an evil woman and still puts up with me! And her assistant, Susan James, who keeps us all sane. Also a very big thank-you for my readers whose letters kept me going. Without you, especially, I wouldn't have come this far. Hugs and kisses for all of you.

ISBN 0-373-16627-3

TWIST OF FATE

Chapter One

"Excuse me, Mr. Gourmet Chef, but am I gonna get those fries soon or would I get them faster if I go down the street to McDonald's? Now *they* know how to get food ready on a timely basis."

"You got a smart mouth, Allie," the cook growled, as he slammed a platter on the counter. "One day it's going to get you into trouble."

"Not in this lifetime, honey." Allie picked up the platter and, juggling it along with a coffeepot, she sashayed across the crowded dining area. Her hot pink waitress uniform and white cotton apron shouldn't have looked sexy, but coupled with Allie's brash beauty and style, it was sizzling. It wasn't because of her glossy black hair, which had been teased up and out to fall in waves past her shoulders. Her eye makeup may have been a bit heavy for daytime wear, but that was Allie, just as no one ever saw her without the bright red lipstick that matched the nail polish on her impossibly long nails. For many in a neighborhood that was rapidly becoming down-and-out, she was one of the few bright spots.

"It's about time you got these here," her customer grumbled as she set the platter next to his hamburger. "They better not be cold."

Allie laughed. "Trust me, honey, those fries are as hot as I am." She deftly evaded his roving hand, which was groping toward her narrow waist and shapely rear, and went to her other tables, pouring coffee at some and writing out bills for others.

She looked up and smiled when a tall man entered the shop, looked around and headed for one of the booths in the back. She snagged a coffee cup from behind the counter and carried it to the booth.

"Hey, handsome." She set the cup down in front of him and filled it with coffee. "What can I do for you?"

He looked up and smiled. "Hey, gorgeous." His smile disappeared when he noticed bruises encircling her wrist. He grasped her hand and looked up. "When are you going to run away with me?"

Allie kept a smile pasted on her lips. "It's no big deal, Pete. Okay?"

Deep gray eyes turned stormy. "It's a big deal if he's hurting you and you know it."

"Don't worry, I can protect myself." She reached inside her apron pocket and pulled out a folded sheet of paper, which she placed in front of him. "Happy birthday!'

"You know very well it's not my birthday." He unfolded the paper and stared at the figures scrawled across it. "How did you get this?"

Allie shrugged. "There was no problem, since Vinnie didn't want a pot of coffee poured in his lap. I just reminded him he owed you for that surveillance job.

He said he'd pay in his own good time and I said he'd pay now. Don't worry. I made sure the check was good."

Pete shook his head. "You should be working collections instead of here."

"Yeah, but the clientele would only be worse." She pulled out her order pad. "The usual?"

He nodded as he smothered a yawn.

Allie looked concerned. "The Anderson divorce?" She chuckled when she saw his warning look. "Honey, everyone knows they're getting divorced and she's convinced he has someone on the side. Thing is, the guy's working two jobs. He doesn't have any time to fool around on her. Here, drink your coffee. I'll be back with your food in no time." She bounced off.

Pete watched Allie head for the counter, drop off his order and move around the restaurant, checking her customers.

Some days he had trouble realizing she was his age. Other days he had trouble believing she could love a sleaze like Whit Richards. He'd busted the guy enough times when he was on the force to know just what kind of man Whit was. And he didn't think much of him. He only wished he could have hung something on the bastard that would have kept him in jail for a long time. One thing he did know—if Richards ever truly hurt Allie, the man would be gumming his food for the rest of his miserable life.

He glanced at the check and shook his head in amazement. He'd been hounding Vinnie for months for the money owed him. Allie made one not-so-idle threat and Pete had his money. Good thing, since his rent was due and Judi had been hinting it would be nice if she was paid on time. For once.

The life of a private investigator wasn't anything like they showed on TV or in the movies. Except that the P.I. was usually short of money. Still, while a regular paycheck from the city had been nice, working for himself meant no following rules when they didn't do any good.

"Here you go, handsome." A platter filled with hash browns, crispy bacon, three eggs, over easy, and a plate of butter-topped toast was set in front of him along with the morning newspaper. "Now eat up."

Pete reached out and snagged the waitress's wrist, careful with his grip as he kept her standing by the table. "Hey, Allie. If you could do anything you wanted to change your life, what would it be?"

Her smile was pure sunshine. "Oh, sweetie, that's easy." She reached down and turned the pages until she reached the society columns. She pointed to a picture taken at a local charity function. "See this picture? I'd be her. She's beautiful, she's got money, a gorgeous fiancé and no problems. I want her life."

"Allie, you're beautiful, too," he protested. "Besides, who says she doesn't have headaches? Having money doesn't mean you have a life without problems."

"Sure it does." She pressed her fingertips against her lips, then against his forehead—another ritual between the old friends. "Now eat up before your food gets cold."

"Allie." He verbally halted her. "I mean it. If he ever hurts you, I want you to come to me."

Allie's smile wobbled. "Hey, I'm fine. Honest."

ALLIE DIDN'T FEEL SO FINE as she walked home to her apartment on feet that felt as if they were on fire. Because another waitress had called in sick, she'd worked a double shift. The idea of a long hot bath sounded like heaven.

"Your rent is late." A woman wearing a flowered housecoat that had seen better days halted Allie's ascent up the stairs.

"Wait a minute, Miss Curtis. Whit told me he gave you the rent a week ago," she argued.

"Your boyfriend hasn't paid me one cent and you know it." The woman spoke around the cigarette sticking out of her mouth. "I want my money."

"All right! You'll get it, but you'll have to wait until tomorrow, when I get paid." She was going to kill Whit when he got home.

"You better pay or you'll be out on the street," Miss Curtis threatened before storming back into her apartment and slamming the door.

"As if that would be a fate worse than death," Allie drawled, making a face at the door. She wrinkled her nose at the strong smell of onions mixed with various odors she didn't care to identify. Whit had promised they would be out of this dump by the end of the month. Trouble was, month end was two days away and he hadn't said anything more about moving.

She looked up the stairs and groaned at the idea of climbing three flights. She slipped off her shoes and wearily held on to the banister as she climbed up. For once, if Whit had the idea of going out, she was going to turn him down. Her feet hurt too much to spend the night dancing, even if it was one of her favorite activities.

When she reached her floor she was surprised to find the overhead light out. Swearing softly, she walked down the dim hallway until she reached the last door. She was surprised to see a pool of light streaming out into the hall because it was ajar.

Allie couldn't imagine a burglar stupid enough to choose her apartment, since there wasn't all that much to steal. And Whit would still be at work. Unless he'd lost this job, too. Just in case, she tiptoed down the hallway.

"I'm telling you I've got good stuff." She was startled to hear her boyfriend's voice. "Have I ever led you wrong before?" He paused, which told her he must be talking on the phone. "No, you can't come here. My old lady could be home at any time and she'd freak out if she knew I was dealing again. Yeah, I can be there in about twenty minutes. See you there."

Allie was positive the color red flashed before her eyes. She didn't want to think about what she was hearing. *That bastard!* Without pausing, she charged inside and threw her purse at him. He had no warning and didn't have time to duck before it bounced off his head.

"You bastard, you promised you wouldn't deal anymore!" she screamed, running at him with her fingers turned into claws.

Whit was handsome in his own way, but there was no doubt his hard life was rapidly taking his looks from him. He immediately sidestepped to avoid her attack. When she turned toward him, his arm swept out and he hit her across the face with the back of his hand.

"Hey, what do you think buys the goodies around here?" he snarled, reaching out and grabbing hold of her uniform front. Two buttons popped and flew into the air. "That crappy job I had? No way, baby."

"Miss Curtis already told me you didn't pay the rent," she snarled back, not the least afraid of him. "So where's the money going?"

"I'll worry about that. This score is going to give us more than enough cash to get out of this hellhole." He shook her so hard her head snapped back and forth.

"Not by dealing drugs," she argued.

"And you're not telling anyone. Especially that SOB Hackett," he warned.

Allie ignored the sound of rending fabric as she freed herself from his grip. "You know how I feel about drugs." She headed for the door. "That's it. You're outta here."

Before she could take a step, she was grabbed from behind and backhanded again. Allie screeched and fought back as she stretched her body in an attempt to reach the phone. Whit cursed loudly as he pulled her back and snatched the phone out of her hand. He threw it across the room, where it slammed against the wall and fell to the floor with a loud dinging sound.

"You know, I'm sick and tired of your goody-two-shoes manner," he muttered.

Allie was past reasoning and raised her knee. There was no way she was going to allow him to win this battle. His scream of pain told her her knee found its target. But even then he didn't let go of her.

"You bitch!" His handsome face turned ugly with rage as he reached inside his shirt. "I gotta say you've been a pain in the ass from the beginning. I only kept you around 'cause you were so good in the sack. I don't need this crap."

Allie tasted the coppery flavor of fear as she spied the knife in his hand. It seemed to move in slow motion toward her. Before she could utter a word, she felt a sharp pain in her chest, then a cold feeling invade her body. Just as suddenly the cold disappeared and a damp warmth flooded her skin. She looked down to see her blood flowing freely down her chest. She looked back up at Whit. She was too stunned to react. For a moment, his anger receded and fear started to take over. Just as rapidly, it disappeared.

"Now maybe you'll know I mean business," he said cockily, although white lines appeared at the edges of his mouth when he realized how serious her injury was.

"*No!*" she whispered as she saw her surroundings seem to grow foggy and eventually turn black.

This isn't fair! she raged as the darkness surrounded her. *He shouldn't be allowed to get away with this. Please, don't let this happen!*

As if her heartfelt plea had been heard, the darkness seemed to fade to a misty gray fog. She still couldn't see anything, but she sensed a presence with her.

Do you want another chance? the presence asked, the unisex voice seeming to come from inside her head.

Yes.

You may have to take on a problem even greater than your own.

I don't care, she heard her own voice answer, an echo inside her head.

Then it shall be.

"BRIANNE. BRIANNE! My God, what have you done?"

When Allie opened her eyes, she knew instantly that something was very different. Not just with her surroundings; her body felt different, too.

First of all, she didn't feel any pain in her chest, only in her head, which ached abominably. Next, she realized she was standing on a very soft carpet. That alone told her she wasn't in her apartment. The beautifully dressed woman standing next to her, wearing a shocked expression, wasn't anyone she knew. Then she felt the metal in her hand and looked down. That was when she saw the lethal-looking handgun. She was not only holding a weapon, but lying at her feet was a man dressed in a tuxedo. What caught her attention was the bright blossom of red flowering on his chest. There was no doubt in her mind that the color wasn't there because he'd spilled catsup on himself!

"Brianne!"

Allie realized the woman was talking to her. She unsteadily rose to her feet, and when she turned, she saw a mirror on the wall behind the woman. The reflection staring back at her was more than a surprise. It was a shock that shook her to her toes.

She felt like Allie. She thought like Allie. The trouble was, she didn't look like Allie.

Instead of glossy black curls flowing to her shoulders, ash blond hair was pulled back in a French twist, with tendrils straggling across her pale cheeks. A white-and-silver, strapless gown covered her slender body instead of a pink waitress uniform that had seen better days. She was positive she could see her own reflection in the mirror, but it looked like a faint memory in the background.

What the hell was going on?

"Brianne, what happened here?" The woman grabbed her arm and pulled her around. "What have you done?"

That was when Allie realized for certain the woman was speaking to her. And that she wasn't Allie Walker any longer. She looked just like the socialite she had pointed out to Pete. The one she told him she wanted to be... Brianne Sinclair.

"Oh boy."

Chapter Two

Allie needed time to think. She needed time to figure out what had happened. And that couldn't be done as long as this woman kept asking questions she couldn't answer. Luckily, her brain stepped in and told her there was only one thing to do: she gasped and fell to the floor in a graceful heap in a faint worthy of an Academy Award.

"She fainted!" the woman cried. "Do you think we should call Dr. Hathaway? Oh, Trey, what happened here?"

"How the hell do I know?" he said, exasperated.

"What are we going to do?" she asked in a shrill voice.

"Shut up, Sheila," the man muttered. "The police are on their way. They'll take care of this."

Allie kept her eyes closed as her mind raced at warp speed. There was one thing she knew for sure: she was very definitely not in her own body! She was in the body of the socialite she'd mentioned to Pete that morning. And for some reason, Brianne Sinclair was holding the gun that must have killed the man lying there. She wished she recognized him, but when she'd looked down, she hadn't been able to get past the wound in his chest.

When I said I wouldn't mind being her, I didn't expect it to end up like this! she thought to herself, feeling panic override everything else.

The strident sound of sirens screaming outside the house abruptly silenced the argument between the couple standing over the prone Brianne.

Allie decided this was a good time for her to regain consciousness. She uttered a credible moan and slowly opened her eyes, staring at them with genuine confusion. She had no idea who they were. She hoped the shock of what had just occurred would allow her puzzlement to go unquestioned.

"What happened?" She was stunned to hear a voice that wasn't hers. Her Brooklyn accent was gone and she now had a low, husky voice that made her think of Lauren Bacall. Where had these cultured tones come from?

The man reached down and took her hand. He looked at her other hand, still holding the gun, with distaste marring his picture perfect features. "I'd say it's pretty obvious, Brianne. The residents of Beverly Hills aren't too fond of scandals and it appears you've created a winner here." He grimaced when he heard pounding at the front door and glanced at the woman. "Sheila, get the door."

She looked as if he'd asked her to walk in bare feet across the desert. "That's Leonard's job."

"I don't give a damn whose job it is. Go to the door and let the police in before they batter it down," he muttered between clenched teeth.

Allie stared at the man and wished she hadn't. She couldn't remember ever seeing a colder-looking person. When he stared at her as if she meant absolutely nothing to him, she pretended to wilt and gingerly touched the back of her skull.

Her mind raced with questions. The first being how did she leave her small apartment in Culver City and end up in Beverly Hills?

"My head hurts," she murmured, then suddenly realized she wasn't lying. A headache the size of Texas was rapidly overtaking her.

Trey grasped her forearm in a punishing grip. "For God's sake, don't tell them anything," he ordered in a low voice. "Use that so-called headache of yours to hold them off. We'll get through this as long as you remain calm. Mother will have a stroke if this blows up in our face."

Allie decided she didn't like him one bit. "I don't think you have to worry, since I don't know what the hell is going on."

He reared back as if she'd thrown off all her clothes. She suddenly realized she must not have been acting the way Brianne Sinclair would.

Could someone please tell me what's happening? she screamed inside her head. Unfortunately, she didn't receive an answer.

ALLIE INSTINCTIVELY STIFFENED when two uniformed officers entered the room.

"Officers, thank you for coming so swiftly." Trey walked over, his hand outstretched as if they were here on a social call.

Both men ignored his hand and focused on the body. The moment they saw the gun in Brianne's hand, they swiftly placed their hands on their own weapons.

"Ma'am, if you would just please hand over the gun," the older officer advised. He glanced at his partner, who was using the small radio hooked to his shoulder to call in a request for a coroner. And a homicide detective.

Allie, you are in so much trouble it isn't funny, she told herself.

"My sister requires medical attention," Trey said imperiously.

Okay, that clears up one question. He's Brianne's brother, she thought, too busy trying to sort things out in her mind to bother listening to the murmured conversation around her. *But is anyone going to explain Sheila? And who the dead man is?*

It seemed only seconds before two men in suits arrived, with the crime-scene unit right behind them.

Allie recognized one of the men as Rick Coffey, Pete's ex-partner. She started to rise to her feet and greet him, but luckily caught herself in time. She doubted Brianne Sinclair would know Rick.

"Miss Sinclair, I'm Sergeant Coffey." Pete's ex-partner walked up and offered his hand. "Is there a quiet place where we can go and talk?"

She looked lost for a moment.

"My sister is suffering from a head injury," Trey interjected. "She really should have immediate medical treatment."

Rick looked up. "Mr. Sinclair," he said with a hint of distaste in his voice. "I am trying to conduct what appears to be a homicide investigation here."

"Is my sister under suspicion?" he demanded.

Rick took a deep breath. "It appears she was found by the body and she was holding the gun. Naturally, I need to find out what she knows."

Trey stood stiffly by Brianne's side. "Then I insist on being present during the questioning."

"Trey." She looked up. "I think it would be better if the detective and I talked alone." She added a smile for reassurance. "Please."

He looked as if he wanted to disagree, but merely nodded and moved away.

"Now, Miss Sinclair." Rick pulled out a notebook and opened it. "Why don't you tell us what happened?"

She took a deep breath. *What are you going to tell him, Allie? That you're not really Brianne Sinclair, even if you look like her? That Whit killed you and you somehow bounced into Brianne Sinclair's body moments after the murder, so you have no idea who did it? Or why you just happened to be holding the gun. And after you're finished with that story, he'll call in the men with white coats, who will take you off to a room with mattresses attached to the walls, where they'll keep you on a steady diet of happy juice.*

She dredged up a faint smile. "I know this sounds incredible, Detective, but I have no idea what happened," she replied. "I don't know if I blacked out or what. I just know that..." She managed a brief smile. "I'm sorry. I have no idea what happened."

One of the crime-scene technicians called out to Rick. He quietly excused himself and walked over to the woman. They carried on a low conversation while Brianne tried very hard not to sit there and fidget. What she wouldn't give for a cigarette! The memory of an article about Brianne Sinclair and the vehement antismoking campaign she'd supported came to mind.

Talk about a hell of a way to quit, she thought to herself, staring down at her fingers intertwined in her lap. No long, red-polished nails for Brianne. The shorter-length nails had been given a French manicure; the hands were soft and well cared for. They belonged to a woman who had never done even a moment's physical labor in her life. Were they hands that would pull a trigger and end a man's life? Try as she might, she didn't think so.

Killing required passion, and Allie couldn't imagine Brianne having that passion within her.

"Miss Sinclair?"

She looked up and found Rick looking at her with an expression that didn't bode well for her. He pulled a small white card out of his wallet and began reading, "You have the right to remain silent."

ALLIE/BRIANNE ENDURED the humiliation of being fingerprinted, having her picture taken and being escorted to a cell.

All because there was proof she had shot what's-his-name, she grumbled silently.

"When I said I wanted to be her, I didn't mean I *literally* wanted to be her. I just wanted the goodies she had. Not the nasties," she groused to herself, settling on the cot. She wrinkled her nose at the unpleasant aromas of urine, body odor and other unidentifiable substances that invaded her cell. "I especially don't care to be her when she's been accused of murdering her fiancé. There's gotta be easier ways of breaking off an engagement than shooting the guy." She crossed her legs, swinging the top one and staring at the leather, wedge-heeled shoe on her foot. She was grateful Rick had allowed her to change into something more suitable before he brought her downtown. She doubted the delicate fabric of the evening gown she'd been wearing would have survived.

"Don't worry," Trey had assured her as she was escorted outside to a waiting patrol car. "I have a call in to Joshua. He'll get you out right away."

Four hours later, she was still waiting for Joshua, the family attorney. She raised her eyes to the ceiling.

"I wish someone would tell me what is going on."

What do you wish to know?

She looked around but couldn't find any evidence of another person in the cell with her. She jumped up and ran to the bars, but didn't see anyone in the hallway, either.

"Did someone say something?" she whispered, gripping the cold metal bars. Her gaze darted back and forth, but she couldn't see even a shadow indicating someone was nearby.

I did.

She released the bars as if they had just emitted an electric charge.

"Now I know I'm losing my mind," she moaned, collapsing back on the cot. "It won't take much. All I have to do is tell the judge I hear voices in my head and he'll make sure I never return to the real world."

If you'll remain quiet and listen to me, I'll be only too happy to explain everything.

She nodded. Why not? She didn't have any other leads. "Okay, go ahead. First of all, what's your name?"

I don't think that's important right now.

She was surprised. The voice didn't give any clue whether it was male or female. "Everyone has a name."

Where I am, I don't need one.

Brianne shrugged and scooted back on the cot, curling her legs under her body. "Where are you?"

In a place you shouldn't have to worry about for a long time. Now, if you're through with the questions, I can get to the business at hand.

"Business at hand?" She laughed. "Honey, my boyfriend stabbed me, I died and for some crazy reason I ended up in another woman's body. Not just any woman, but one now accused of murder. You couldn't have picked someone with better prospects?"

You were the one who chose Brianne Sinclair, not me. Remember?

She threw up her hands. "You must have known I don't have a great track record in picking people. Whit was the perfect example."

Perfect is not a word I would use to describe that creature. I wouldn't worry if I were you. All you have to do is prove Brianne innocent—and I can assure you she's not guilty. With the right kind of help, you'll be able to accomplish that.

She sat up at that announcement. "How can I prove she's innocent? She was standing there holding the gun that obviously killed her fiancé."

That's up to you.

She waved her forefinger in the air. "Okay, if I do it, what happens next? I mean, I'm dead, so I can't go back to being Allie. Is this going to be a regular thing for me? I mean, am I going to start bouncing around to different bodies of people who need help?"

Please, Brianne, this is reality, not television.

"Terrific, a voice with an attitude," she muttered. "Well, I'm not talking to anyone who doesn't have a name. Can I call you Al?"

Not if you want me to answer you. All you have to remember is that you are now Brianne Sinclair. Allie Walker is no longer among us. Which means you have to act accordingly.

"But I don't know anything about her life!" she argued.

Don't worry, I'll help you with that.

"But if you don't have a name, how am I supposed to call you? How about a pager number?" She couldn't resist the sarcasm.

I'll know when you need me. Now, just remember you're Brianne. I'll be in touch.

She jumped up. "Wait a minute!"

"Will you shut up!" a voice yelled from one of the other cells.

Brianne waited, vainly listening for the voice in her head to return. But there was nothing. She stretched out on the cot, grimacing at the rough blanket beneath her.

"Great, there's no way a high-priced lawyer is going to be able to help me out of this mess," she muttered. "I'm going to have to get someone of my own to help." As she closed her eyes, the name of that someone came to mind.

PETE STARED AT THE TWO paragraphs hidden in a corner on page eight of the paper.

Waitress Killed During Burglary. Boyfriend Badly Beaten.

His reaction to the article was a string of profanities that would make a sailor blush.

"That bastard did it," he muttered, tossing the paper onto his desk, which was littered with paper cups half-filled with coffee, a partially eaten Danish that was now rock hard and four empty beer bottles.

The more he sat there and brooded, the more his thoughts turned to dangerous pursuits. Muttering another string of curses, he stood up and pulled on his battered black leather jacket over a rumpled khaki-colored cotton shirt and worn jeans.

"Hey, Judi, I'm going out for a while," he told his secretary as he passed her desk.

She didn't look up. It was apparent that polishing her nails a brilliant fuchsia was much more important than anything he said.

"Doing what?" she asked idly.

"Leaning on a suspect."

"In case you forgot, you're not allowed to do that anymore." She carefully dragged the brush across her forefinger, then painted the sides of the nail. "Detective Coffey said if you did it again he'd throw you in jail and forget you were there. And while you might not mind taking a county-paid vacation, I'd really prefer you didn't so I could get my paycheck on time."

Pete grinned. "When was the last time you got paid on time?"

She pretended to think about it. "Last year."

"Don't worry, Rick won't mind if I have a talk with this guy," Pete said with a grim smile.

Judi's own smile dimmed as she realized the direction of his thoughts. "You're going to talk to that creep, Whit, aren't you?"

"Better you don't know."

Her eyes, a cobalt blue thanks to contact lenses, narrowed. "Give him one for me, Pete."

"Will do. Just as soon as I finish giving him my opinion." He pulled open the door and stalked out.

Pete took the elevator down to the underground parking lot where he kept his aging Porsche. By all rights, he should have gotten rid of the damn car years ago, but he figured he'd worked his ass off to pay for it, and by God, he intended to keep the baby until either it or he fell apart.

It wasn't difficult to figure out where he'd find Whit. All he had to do was locate a crap game and he knew the lowlife would be in the middle of it.

It turned out he was right. Whit was there, with a blonde wearing the shortest and tightest skirt Pete had ever seen on a woman, a brief top that looked more like a Band-Aid barely covering her ample breasts. He wondered how she managed to walk down the street without getting arrested.

"Hey, Whit, how ya doin'?" Pete slung a companionable arm around the slighter man's shoulders. "Man, you've been through hell. First the love of your life is killed in that ugly way, then you're beaten up. I gotta give you a lot of credit. You seem to be holding up pretty well after the tragedy.'' He glanced at the woman, who offered him a warm smile. ''I bet this little cupcake is helping you cope with your sorrow, huh? I bet she's helping a lot.''

The other man eyed him warily. ''What's it to you?''

''Oh, it's a lot to me.'' Pete gestured toward Whit's face, which was marred with bruises and a black eye. ''I have to say your buddies did a good job of working you over. How much you hafta pay them for the roughing up? Hell, you should've asked me. I would have been more than happy to do it for free.'' His dark gray eyes turned to the color of steel.

Whit tried to shrug off his arm, but Pete merely tightened his hold. His thumb found a crucial nerve and pressed down. The other man whimpered, but was sensible enough not to fight him.

''Hey, I went through hell that night,'' Whit whined. ''First someone breaking into the apartment, then killing Allie and beating me up because I tried to fight them off. It hasn't been easy for me.''

Pete leaned down and whispered in his ear. ''Yeah, funny thing about how that all happened, isn't it? I'm still trying to figure out why they killed Allie but only beat you.'' He shook his head, clucking his tongue. ''You know what, Whit? That story of yours stinks like last week's fish. And if there's something I can tell, it's a bad story, and yours is about the worst I've heard in a long time.'' Keeping his arm around Whit, he dragged the man over to one side. ''I only have a couple questions. Why in the hell would they kill a sweetheart like Allie and leave scum like you alive? Anyone with a reasonable mind would have knifed you and just knocked her around. Does that make any sense to you?''

The man's face turned white under the black-and-purple bruises. ''You don't leave me alone, Hackett, I'll call the cops and tell them you're harassing me.''

''Yeah, I just bet they'd love to hear that from you.'' Pete backed Whit up against a wall. He placed his forearm against his throat, pressing down just enough to partially block his oxygen intake. Pete's body vibrated with angry energy that he barely kept under control. He wanted the man scared senseless. ''Listen carefully, Whit, because I don't intend to repeat myself. I know you killed Allie,'' he said in a fierce whisper, putting his face close to Whit's. ''And I'm going to get to the truth. One way or another, I'm going to prove you killed her, and when I do I'm going to make sure they throw your sorry ass in jail and that you don't get out until you're a very old man. Of course, that's if there's anything left after I finish with you.'' He bared his teeth in a shark's smile. ''Ya know, Whit, they're gonna love that pretty face of yours in prison.''

Fear flashed briefly in the man's eyes, although he put on a tough front. ''Don't even try threatening me, Hackett.''

Pete straightened up and sauntered toward the door. ''Hell, Whit, I'm not threatening you. I'm making a promise.'' He opened the door and looked back over his shoulder. ''You know, there's this word that rhymes with your name, which I feel describes you to a tee.'' He sketched a salute and walked out, closing the door on Whit's curses.

Pete walked back toward his car, his hands pushed deep in his jeans pockets. He nodded at one of the hookers who stood on the nearby corner.

"Hey, Pete, when are you going to let me show you what you need?" she called after him, wiggling her rear end in a saucy manner.

"Sorry, Mona, I don't think I could handle it," he teased. Then he grew sober. "When you going to bail out?"

Her smile didn't reach her eyes. "It's too late, honey." Her gaze, appreciating him for the solid male he was, watched him continue on to his car.

Pete wasn't drop-dead handsome, but he had an air about him that attracted women like flies. He'd understood it when he had been a cop. Cop groupies were the bane, and reward, of a cop's life.

Six feet tall with a lanky build, sandy brown hair that always seemed to need a trim and stormy gray eyes that saw it all, he felt he was nothing special. He didn't have a lot of money to attract a woman and he knew he never would. That was fine. He was content with what he had, which amounted to a twenty-four-year-old Porsche, a business that was in the red more than the black, and the right to call his life his own. No more answering to lieutenants who believed in doing everything by the book when Pete knew there were times that didn't accomplish a damn thing. After fifteen years on the force, arresting scum who were out on the street the following day, he'd finally handed in his resignation and worked on getting his P.I. license. While the money wasn't steady, he could at least call his life his own.

Right now, he was glad for that freedom, because that meant he could keep an eye on Whit. The bastard had killed Allie, and Pete intended to find the proof. He climbed behind the wheel of his Porsche and started up the engine. The throaty purr of the classic machine soothed him as his thoughts returned to Allie.

"You know why the women are always after you, sweetie?" she used to tell him. "Because while you look safe, they sense you aren't, and that's as good as catnip to a cat. They like that aura of danger you exude."

"Dammit, Allie." He shifted gears with a savage gesture. Unfamiliar tears burned his eyes. "Why the hell didn't you leave that bastard when I asked you to?"

"YOUR HONOR, my client has strong ties to the community, both social and business, and shouldn't be considered a flight risk," Joshua Randolph argued persuasively. "Her mother is an invalid, and Miss Sinclair wouldn't dream of abandoning her."

The judge looked bored with the proceedings. "It wouldn't be the first time an adoring daughter left Mom behind, Counselor. The defendant will surrender her passport."

He named a bail that made Brianne blink more than once. But her attorney merely nodded, as if the large amount was commonplace.

Of course, it's nothing to him, she said to herself. *You're rich now and don't have to buy anything that smacks of generic. Hell, you can even send someone else out to do the shopping!*

Joshua turned to her with a smug smile on his patrician lips. "Don't worry, my dear." He picked up her hand and patted it. "This will soon work out. No one will believe you would have harmed one hair on Michael's head."

"Considering the amount of evidence they say they have against me, I wonder if I shouldn't look for some evidence on my side," she said wryly.

"That isn't something for you to worry about. I'll hire the best investigators to clear you," he assured her.

Something popped into her mind. "If you don't mind, I think I'll take care of that point." She smiled at him and walked out of the courtroom.

It was no surprise that the news media was waiting in force. Trey took her arm and guided her through the throng, shouting, "No comment!" to all questions.

Brianne was handed into the back of a waiting limo and Trey climbed in after her.

"Why did you tell Joshua you'd take care of the investigation? He's an excellent attorney," he argued.

"An excellent corporate attorney." *Now, how did she know that?* "He knows nothing about criminal law. I want an investigator who's worked with criminals and I want a top-notch criminal attorney." She stared at Trey. Something told her he was used to getting his way with his sister, and his look of surprise was due to his sibling now standing up to him. Little did he know that Allie didn't back down to anyone! She raised her chin an extra inch. "Are we clear on this?"

Trey studied her with a narrowed gaze. "Something's happened to you since last night. You're not the same." He suddenly stiffened. "Did something happen while you were in jail?"

Brianne rolled her eyes. "You've watched too many prison movies, Trey. I had a lovely cell all to myself." *And a voice with an attitude,* she mentally amended. "I just realize that what happened is very serious and I need to do something."

"Then let Joshua take care of this."

She met his gaze. "I prefer to take care of it myself."

She was positive that Trey's petulant expression wasn't anything new to Brianne. She hid the smile blossoming inside her. Little did he know that dealing with Allie would be an altogether different story!

Chapter Three

Pete walked past rows of battered, gray metal desks set up for the homicide detectives. He noticed nothing had changed in the time he had been gone. The place still smelled of sweat, fear and frustration. There were no muted voices here, but a babble of noise as interrogations went on, reports were written up and phone calls made.

"Anyone see the Henderson file?" one man shouted. "Dammit, I need that file!"

"I don't care what his attorney says, he's guilty as hell," another said into the phone he had cradled between chin and shoulder as he doodled sketches of buxom naked women on a notepad.

Several detectives looked up and waved at Pete or flipped him the finger.

Pete sketched a mocking bow. "Thank you, thank you. It's always nice to know who my friends are."

He walked on until he reached one of the rear desks, where his ex-partner, Rick Coffey, sat. The man was leaning back in his chair, drinking what Pete was positive was cold coffee. Rick looked up.

"Damn, Hackett, you look old."

Pete's retort was predictably profane. "And to think I went to great trouble to bring decent coffee in here for you." He set a tall plastic cup in front of him.

Rick pulled off the top and inhaled the aroma of the steaming contents. "If it wasn't for this I'd throw you out on your ass," he muttered, sipping the hot brew.

"If it wasn't for me, you wouldn't have the best seat in the house," Pete quipped, gesturing toward the crowded room.

"So what brings you slumming?"

Pete perched himself on the edge of Rick's desk. "Allie Walker's murder."

Rick grimaced. He couldn't count the number of meals he'd eaten at the coffee shop where she'd worked. "No suspects."

"Whit Richards," Pete countered.

"Then Whit took a hell of a beating for killing her."

Pete shot him a wry look. "Get real, Coffey. You can't tell me you believe somebody broke into their apartment, killed Allie for no reason and only beat up scum like Richards."

"No, I don't, but I can't find any proof he did it." Rick gave a sigh. "Look, pal, Allie was fantastic. A good friend to all us cops. But there's no way Richards would have been stupid enough to kill her. He knows how much we all liked her and that we'd do everything we could to find her killer. Trouble is, we can't pin it on him, as much as we'd all like to."

"That's only because he was fast enough to get some of his buddies to cover his tracks by beating him up," he argued. "It makes perfect sense and you know it."

Rick shook his head. "Hey, I know what you're saying, but we have zip. And right now the mayor is on my ass because of Brianne Sinclair offing her fiancé." He shook his head. "Gee, and I thought all you had to do was give back the ring. They want a conviction in this case, but some points are a little murky and it's up to me to make them come out loud and clear."

"Yeah, I read about it." Pete looked down at his hands. There was nothing memorable about them except they used to hold a gun more than he liked. "Funny thing, the day Allie died, she said she wouldn't mind living Brianne Sinclair's life. That she wouldn't have any worries if she was her."

"Yeah, well, Allie should be glad she isn't Sinclair, because if justice works the way it should, that woman's going to be growing old in a prison cell unless her high-priced lawyer gets her off," Rick replied sardonically. "And considering the amount of money he'll be making off this case and the power the Sinclair name holds in this town, I'd say she'll go free. If she's smart, she won't get engaged again anytime soon."

"I want anything you have on Allie's case," Pete said.

Rick looked at him as if he had just asked for a million dollars. "You know very well I can't do that."

"It's never stopped you before."

Rick leaned forward and whispered fiercely, "Okay, fine, we all know Richards killed Allie, but there's no proof. Trust me, I checked this out carefully. There's a lot of us cops who're going to miss her and want to see her killer brought in, but I have to play by the book."

Pete stood up. "I don't."

"Dammit, Pete, don't do anything stupid!"

He shook his head. "I don't intend to, but I'm not going to see Richards get away with Allie's murder. I owe her that." He started to walk away.

"You find anything, you bring it to me first," Rick shouted after him.

Pete didn't answer. He merely waved his hand over his head as he made his way through the obstacle course of desks.

Rick dropped back into his seat. "Damn."

"ISN'T THERE ANYTHING you can tell me? Just give me a hint!" Brianne paced her opulent, Wedgwood blue and antique cream bedroom. She hated it—the delicate, French antique furniture, the pale colors, even the plush cream-colored carpet. She hated pastels. She felt they were always pale and insipid. All the decor did was depress her.

When Trey dropped her off at the mansion before heading downtown to the family-owned department store, he had advised her to relax in a hot tub. Thanks to subtle messages in her mind, she found her way to her bedroom without asking for directions. A maid named Lucille appeared and offered to draw her a bath and lay out a change of clothing. Brianne discovered a closet that was larger than Allie's apartment, filled with every description of clothing and accessories. A small wall safe in the back held jewelry—not a single costume piece among it.

Brianne spent an hour luxuriating in a bubble-filled tub large enough for three people. By the time she got out she felt one hundred percent better. She dismissed Lucille's hovering by explaining she wished to rest.

"Hello! Are you there?" she called out in a soft voice the minute she was alone.

You really must learn some discretion, my dear.

She dropped into a blue-silk, cushioned chair. "Terrific. I'm going on trial for murder and you're giving me etiquette lessons. Have you looked at this place? The woman had no taste."

She was on every best-dressed list in the country.

"All the best-dressed socialites shop at Dowagers R Us," she muttered. "Everything in her closet is white, cream, beige or black. The black I can handle, but the other stuff is like eating whipped cream. The woman needs color in her life!"

Careful.

She shook her head. "There's no one here but me."

Tell me something I don't know.

Brianne threw her hands up. "I don't want to go back to jail! Last night was not a pleasant experience."

You told Brianne's brother you were going to hire your own legal assistance. You have the funds available, so do it.

"You really have an attitude," she groused.

If I do it's because I deal with mortals like you. I would like to make another suggestion. Brianne Sinclair's checkbook is in the top desk drawer. You should sit down and learn how to sign her name.

She wrinkled her nose. "Tell me one thing. What happened to the real Brianne?"

She wasn't strong enough to handle the death of her fiancé.

"That's it?"

That's all you need to know for now.

"And here I thought she had everything." Brianne got up and moved over to the bed, dropping down on the silk comforter. The fabric was cool on her skin.

It wasn't long before the past twelve hours caught up with her and she fell asleep. Just as she drifted off, a name came to mind. The name of someone she knew could help her. The name of the only person she knew she could trust.

"At least I can make sure he pays his rent for the next year," she murmured drowsily.

CLASSY RED BMW convertibles didn't travel through Pete's neighborhood. Not unless they were stolen. He took note of the license plate as he walked past the car and into his office building.

"You have a client in your office," Judi informed him as he entered. "So don't blow it. Show her some of that charm you keep so well hidden."

He held out his arms in the classic pose of innocence.

"She's loaded," Judi added.

He glanced through the mail on the desk—all bills he had to figure out how to pay. "What'd you do, run a credit check on the lady?"

"Didn't have to. The clothes she's wearing cost more than I make in three months. At least, what I would make in three months if I got paid on time."

Knowing she wasn't about to tell him anything more, Pete dropped the envelopes on her desk and headed for his office.

The moment he stepped inside, he knew what Judi meant. The scent of French perfume reached his nostrils first. Then the woman came into view.

Her pictures didn't do her justice. Ash blond hair was pulled back in a French braid and secured with a black velvet bow. Her linen dress was black, very simple, but costly. Her legs were clad in black stockings and she wore black high heels. She was seated in the visitor's chair, fidgeting a bit as if she was unsure what to do.

The grieving fiancée, he thought sardonically. "If I were Bogart I'd be asking what a classy dame like you is doing in a hellhole like this."

She turned around and looked at him with the largest, greenest eyes he'd ever seen. If she hadn't already been branded a killer, he would have decided he was most definitely in love.

Pete was puzzled by her reaction. For a split second the expression in her eyes was that of greeting, as if she knew him. Just as quickly, it was masked and she stood up.

"Mr. Hackett." She held out her hand.

Skin smooth as silk thanks to expensive creams didn't flinch from his rougher palm.

"You're a brave woman to drive a BMW down this way." He reluctantly withdrew his hand and walked around his desk. He waited until Brianne seated herself before he sat down. "Cars like yours aren't known to still be in one piece when the owners return."

Her smile was dazzling. "I'll take my chances."

Pete picked up his pencil for lack of anything else to do.

"I want to hire you," she began without preamble. "I'm sure you've heard this before, but it's true. I didn't kill my fiancé. I want you to find the truth behind his death."

"I'm sure your attorney will have his own choice for an investigator. And I'm also sure I'd be at the bottom of the list. If I'm even on it."

"Mr. Hackett, I think we both know that my attorney wouldn't know a criminal if he saw one unless the crime was white collar variety," she candidly stated. "I want someone who knows the criminal mind inside out. Who knows where to look for dirt. You were a cop. A good one."

Pete set his pencil down. "Look, Miss Sinclair. I don't know if this is some kind of joke or if you're just in a slumming mood today, but I don't think I'm the kind of investigator you want. I don't have a fancy office or the resources Beverly Hills investigators would have at their disposal."

"I can arrange for anything you need." Desperation marked her features. "I don't want some yes man to handle my case. I want someone who will put his all into finding the truth. And I know you will." She glanced over to the file cabinet, where a newspaper article was taped to the top drawer.

Waitress Killed During Burglary was the headline.

Something he couldn't quite read briefly crossed her features and she looked as if she flinched. When she turned back to him, her expression was bland as milk.

"I realize you are an honorable man," she said huskily. "And that's what I need. An honorable man."

"Obviously expense is no object for you?"

"I want the truth, Mr. Hackett."

Pete leaned back in his chair. He reflectively rubbed his chin as he studied her. She didn't flinch from his regard or look away.

His instincts told him the best thing to do was tell her he couldn't take her case. He could even give her several names of reputable investigators who could help her. But something held him back. He wasn't sure what it was, only that he felt this was a case he couldn't afford to turn away.

Plus, he told himself, the money would come in handy for his work on Allie's case.

He named a figure. "That's daily and, of course, there's always expenses."

She nodded as she pulled out a checkbook. "Two weeks in advance and we can take it from there?" She began writing. "I also want to know everything you find out." She tore the check out and handed it to him.

Pete didn't faint as he glanced at the numbers written on the check. He carefully folded it and slipped it inside his shirt pocket. "I'll send you updates."

"No, I want to be there." She looked as if she wasn't going to budge.

He figured he'd argue that point later. "Before we can do that, I need some information from you." He pulled a lined legal pad out of his desk drawer and started scrawling across the top sheet. "First off, were there any problems between you and your fiancé?"

"No."

"Did you have an intimate relationship with your fiancé?"

Only a practiced interrogator like Pete would have noticed the slight hesitation before she answered.

"Yes."

For the next ninety minutes, he asked questions and Brianne answered. What puzzled him was the slight hesitation with every answer she gave, as if she was waiting for someone else to answer the question.

"I'll get in touch with the police and ask for copies of their reports," he told her finally. "I admit I'm leery of taking this case, Miss Sinclair. According to everything I've read it's pretty cut-and-dried. Including your guilt."

Her gaze flicked toward the article taped on the file drawer. "Yes, that's what they all say." She stood up and held out her hand. "Thank you, Mr. Hackett."

With her movement, the scent of her perfume drifted in his direction. "One more question."

She looked at him with silent inquiry.

"Why me?"

She took her time replying as she draped the gold chain of her black leather bag over her shoulder. "That was easy. I wanted the best."

Five minutes later, when Judi walked into the office, Pete was still standing, staring at the door.

"Where's her check?" she demanded, holding out her hand.

"Bitch, bitch, bitch," he grumbled good-naturedly, pulling the check out of his shirt pocket and handing it to her. "Here. Are you happy now?"

She unfolded it, stared at the figure and squealed so loudly that Pete winced.

"I'm really going to miss my eardrums," he muttered.

"I want a raise," she announced immediately.

BRIANNE WAS BORED. After spending a couple of hours perfecting the Sinclair heiress's signature, then inspecting her personal belongings to get an idea of what the real Brianne was like, she had come to the conclusion that the woman had led an insular life.

"A boring life," she said out loud as she wandered about the glass-enclosed sunroom. When she returned from Pete's office, she'd been served lunch here, and she'd savored every bite of the delectable chicken salad and warm, buttered rolls. "Okay, I don't have to cook, don't have to worry about guys trying to cop a feel. But at least my own life wasn't this dull."

"Oh, darling, don't tell me one night in that horrible place has you talking to yourself!"

Brianne turned to watch a striking woman cross the room. Golden blond hair hung in loose curls to her shoulders. Her hot-pink linen jacket and skirt that bared her thighs were most definitely haute couture, and her black, high-heeled pumps were Italian leather. Brianne wasn't even going to hazard a guess as to the cost of her jewelry.

"I was so worried about you." The woman enveloped her in a cloud of Chanel as she hugged her and offered an air kiss.

Lisa Winters, Brianne's best friend and head viper.

"Lisa, how nice to see you." She offered the same. "How are you?" *Ask her about Rome.* "How was Rome?"

"I came back with bruises on bruises." Lisa leaned back and searched Brianne's face. "I must say you don't look any the worse for wear. I was stunned to hear about Michael. How dreadful for you. What happened?"

"That's what I'd like to know," she said wryly. She glanced up when a maid stepped into the room, and turned back to Lisa. "Would you care for some coffee?"

"Yes, thank you." Lisa sat on a chair and waited for Brianne to give the maid instructions. "Tell me all about it. They didn't strip-search you, did they?" Vivid blue eyes studied her avidly. "I've heard they're doing that kind of thing now."

"Nothing that exciting," she drawled. "But it was an experience I wouldn't care to repeat. Please, Lisa, I really don't want to talk about it. I'd rather hear about Rome."

It didn't take much persuasion to get the other woman rambling on about parties she had attended, interesting men she had met and seduced and mutual friends she had seen. The more Brianne heard, the more she realized why her "voice" had called Lisa a viper. The woman had a deadly way with words and was obviously a mistress at verbally tearing a person to pieces. Brianne remained content to sit back and nod at the right times. She figured it was a good way to learn more about her so-called friends.

How did Brianne survive in a world like this? she asked herself as she kept her smile firmly pasted on her lips.

Lisa glanced around. "Is Sheila here?"

By now Brianne had learned that Sheila was Trey's wife and her sister-in-law. "She had a hair appointment."

Lisa fingered her diamond bracelet. "Remind me she owes me lunch." She laughed throatily. "We had a wager and I won."

Brianne leaned forward as she knew she was expected to. "What wager?"

"I told her I could get that stuffy old Carlton into bed, and not only that, but he would be wearing a pink bow on a very strategic part of his body." Lisa burst into laughter. "I wish I had taken pictures! It was priceless!"

And I thought socialites were repressed, Brianne thought. *What does she do for an encore?*

It's better you don't know at this time.

Brianne conquered the urge to smile as the voice intruded her mind. She decided her voice-with-an-attitude also had a sense of humor. That she could handle a lot easier.

"I know this is a difficult time for you, but you have to go on with your life," Lisa insisted. "We'll start with lunch out and a round of shopping. You'll be back to yourself in no time."

Brianne looked at her. Lisa's diamond-shaped face went with her diamond-shaped mind. "You don't believe I killed Michael?"

"Of course not!" she replied. "I dislike speaking ill of the dead, but Michael was not the most perfect man in the world. I always felt you could do better. Speaking of Michael, when is his funeral?"

"I have no idea," she said honestly. "Besides, I don't think it would be a good idea for me to attend."

"Of course, it would. Would a guilty person appear?" Liza patted her hand, then leaned forward and lowered her voice. "How is Olivia? Is she feeling any better?"

Your mother spends most of her time in her suite. She's in a wheelchair.

"The same." At least, she hoped the older woman was.

Lisa shook her head. "You've had so much trag-edy in your life, but don't worry. Auntie Lisa is here to liven things up." She flashed a wicked smile.

The Allie part of Brianne had had more than her share of partying, but she had an idea her own choice of parties was nothing compared to the ones Lisa had attended.

"I see the wicked one is back."

The two women turned toward the sunroom door-way. A delicate-looking woman with pale blond hair drawn away from her face negotiated her motorized wheelchair between towering ficus trees. Looking at her face was looking at Brianne's twenty-five years from now.

Her pale pink robe was made of fine cashmere and covered a slight, frail body, but there was a blaze of determination in eyes as green as her daughter's. She lifted long delicate fingers, which trembled slightly, toward the two women. Even with diminished health, Olivia Sinclair was a formidable-looking individual. For a moment Brianne felt as if she should curtsy.

"I understand you enjoyed Rome in your usual manner, Lisa," Olivia said in a voice that was as husky as Brianne's, but like her hand, had a faint tremor. "I do hope you took the proper precautions." Her smile held little humor. "Yes, even I, in my ivory tower, understand the importance of safe sexual relations."

Lisa laughed throatily. "Olivia, you look wonder-ful." She got up and walked over to the woman, pressing a kiss on her cheek. "How are you feeling? I must say you look marvelous. Have you spent time at that spa again?"

Olivia didn't deign to reply. She was too preoccupied with her daughter.

Go over and kiss her, you dolt! Must I tell you everything?

Brianne pulled together a bright smile as she approached her mother.

Okay, Allie, this is one woman you don't call Ma, she reminded herself as she bent at the waist and kissed the older woman's forehead.

"I'm so glad you came down to join us, Mother," she murmured. "Would you like me to ring for some tea?"

Olivia's hand snaked out and grasped her wrist with a grip that was surprisingly strong for all her fragile manner.

"Who are you and where is my daughter?"

Chapter Four

Brianne had to force herself not to step back in obvious defense at Olivia's question, uttered in a demanding tone.

"Honestly, Olivia. I think you should talk to your doctor about adjusting your medication." Lisa's laughter rang out like broken glass. "Even *I* can see that Brianne is standing there right in front of you."

Olivia's cold, penetrating gaze effectively froze Brianne to the spot.

"Yes, of course, she is." The faintest of lights flickered in the older woman's gaze as she briefly turned to the visitor. "How kind of you to point it out to me, Lisa."

Brianne stepped back when Olivia steered her wheelchair forward. The swish of the wheels on the Italian-marble floor was the only sound in the sunroom.

"How is your mother, Lisa?" Olivia asked, stopping when her chair was beside the one Brianne had been sitting in.

"She says she's fine, but this divorce took a lot out of her. Mainly money. Rod decided his six months with her was worth a great deal.'' Lisa dug into her purse and pulled out a bright pink leather case that held her cigarettes. She started to pull one out, then stopped when she saw the look of pained disapproval on Olivia's face. "Sorry, it's a nasty habit I just can't seem to give up. Oh, Brianne, by the way—" she turned back to her friend "—a Sergeant Coffey left a message with my service. He wants to set up an appointment to talk to me." She leaned forward. "Please tell me he's good-looking. Do you think he'll want to interrogate me down at the police station? What would you like me to tell him? That you've always been a saint and wouldn't harm a fly? This is all so deliciously sordid." Her eyes sparkled at the ideas forming in her mind.

"Don't you think you should tell him the truth?" Brianne suggested, hoping the blonde might shed some light on the puzzle she was living in.

Lisa's laughter was still the cutting-glass variety. "The truth! Now that would be something new for me, wouldn't it?" She didn't mind that she was basically insulting herself. "I'm not sure that would be a good idea." She glanced at Olivia. "Darling, you know what I mean."

Olivia's smile could have frozen the arctic circle. "You always did prefer evading the truth, didn't you, dear? It makes it easier for you to travel through life that way."

Lisa's beauty was marred by the fury that briefly crossed her features. "You always do enjoy cutting to the bone, don't you?" she purred. "I guess it's to make up for your... infirmity."

"Lisa!" Brianne was stunned by the vicious statement.

Olivia merely smiled again. "Oh, Brianne, you very well know that Lisa and I have understood each other for years."

"I'm glad someone understands what's going on here," Brianne mumbled, wondering if she'd somehow stumbled onto the Mad Tea Party. The mad part certainly fit.

"It's always so nice to see you, Lisa. You remind me of me." Olivia went on, her smile not wavering.

Lisa arched an eyebrow. "Oh really? I must say that's a high compliment since you've always been a force to be reckoned with." She glanced at her diamond-studded watch and gathered up her purse. "I really should be off. I'm going to the theater with Reese tonight." She offered a deprecating smile. "Yes, I know he's a bore, but I was depressed when he called and I couldn't think of a polite way to say no." She brushed an air kiss past Brianne's cheek, stopped to do the same with Olivia and walked out of the sunroom with Brianne following her. "We have to plan lunch soon." She lowered her voice. "Now, darling, I realize the police are going to find out the truth about Michael sooner or later, so for your own sake, please be careful what you say about him. I don't want to see you end up wearing those dreary prison outfits. They're so unflattering to one's figure and coloring." With another smile that didn't stretch one muscle on her face, she walked out to her car.

Brianne dreaded going back into the sunroom and facing her mother again. She could have kissed the butler when he approached her with a message.

"Miss Sinclair, there is a Mr. Hackett on the telephone," he announced in his formal voice. "I'm afraid he wouldn't tell me his business."

"Thank you, I'll take it upstairs." She hurried up the final staircase, then down the hallway to her suite.

She paused before picking up the phone.

"Good afternoon, Mr. Hackett," she said in measured tones. "Do you have some news for me?"

"More like a question." His voice rumbled in her ear. "Why didn't you tell me the two of you had a big fight at some fancy dinner party two nights before he was killed? Let me tell you, that story is making for juicy telling down at the station. That doesn't make things look good."

She felt her world slip out of her grasp.

"It's not what you think." She made a face as the words left her mouth. Couldn't she have come up with a more original statement?

"Yeah, that's what they all say. Look, no offense, you're a nice lady," he continued. "You'd ordinarily have a good reputation in town if it wasn't for this murder charge hanging over your head, and your check cleared without a hitch. But I'll be honest. With the evidence against you, you don't have a prayer of getting off."

"So you're saying you believe I'm guilty before you do anything more than a preliminary investigation?"

"You were holding the damned gun. That's cut-and-dried to a lot of people. I'd have to say it looks it to me."

Brianne mentally counted to ten. "Are you still at your office?"

"Yeah, but I'm on my way out."

"Wait for me."

"Sorry," he said without apology, "I keep strict hours."

"You cashed my check, so you'll wait." She slammed the phone down and raced for the closet. She quickly changed her clothes and almost ran down the stairs.

"Miss Sinclair?" The butler looked at her questioningly as she hurried past him.

"I won't be in for dinner," she called over her shoulder. *Dammit, I need to find out that man's name!*

His name is Leonard, he's been with the family for thirty years and he's thinking he should start wearing a bulletproof vest.

"That is not funny," she muttered, tossing her purse into the passenger seat and sliding behind the wheel of her car. She had to smile as the engine purred the moment she turned the key. A far cry from her beat-up Chevy, which only started after a round of curses and a few kicks in the right place.

Then we're even, because I don't believe I have ever dealt with anyone as irritating as you are.

Brianne sped up the moment the car cleared the tall, wrought-iron gates that guarded the estate.

"What did I fight with Michael about?" she asked, swiveling her eyes between the rearview and side-view mirrors.

What does any woman engaged to a man fight about?

"Hell if I know. I've never been engaged."

Let's just say that Michael hurt you badly, but no matter what he did to you, you wouldn't have hurt him back in such a violent manner. Violence wasn't part of your emotional makeup.

"I don't think that kind of explanation would stand up in court." She performed a risky zigzag maneuver once she was on the freeway. She was already in love with her car. Something that responded so readily was a treat. Her fingers impatiently tapped the steering wheel as she spied the heavy rush-hour traffic. "'It's this way, your honor. A voice told me I was put in Brianne Sinclair's body because she needed help. And the voice also told me the real Brianne would never shoot her fiancé.' The minute the judge heard that I'd be out the door wearing a very stylish white jacket with lots of buckles, and they'd put me in a padded room and feed me happy pills."

You are not sounding like Brianne Sinclair.

"That's because, inside, I'm not Brianne Sinclair!" She managed a faint smile when a motorist in the lane alongside her stared at her strangely. "Terrific, it's starting already."

I suggest you remember that you are no longer Allie Walker but Brianne Sinclair. You are now the woman you wanted to be and you need to act accordingly.

"Yeah, well, I'd like to change that wish. Maybe to someone who won't be spending the rest of her life in prison."

Too late. I would also suggest you cease this reckless driving or you will end up with a ticket. That would not be a good idea right now, since you wouldn't care to attract any more attention from the police.

She obligingly eased her foot off the accelerator and remained in the lane she had entered. But that didn't stop her from looking for an opportunity to ease her way ahead.

"What am I supposed to tell Pete about the fight?"

I wouldn't worry. I'm sure you'll think of something appropriate.

"I wish you would stop saying that, because I'm worried as hell." She ignored any more internal warnings and shot around two cars as she headed for the off ramp. Within minutes she was parked in front of Pete's building. As she climbed out of her car, she realized he was waiting in the doorway. While he wore his battered, black leather jacket in deference to the chilly weather, it was unzipped. His white cotton shirt visible under the jacket had clearly not seen an iron in its lifetime, and from experience, she knew it never would. Pete didn't believe in putting on airs for any client. Even if her check did clear without a hitch.

Gray eyes with an impeding storm in their depths watched her approach. A flicker of awareness appeared as he studied her from head to toe. Knowledgeable of the neighborhood she was headed for, she had changed into a pair of navy wool pants and a cream-colored, high-necked blouse that she hated, but had found was the plainest item in the closet. Even though her clothing was simple, it was obviously expensive. She made a mental note to do some shopping. She couldn't handle wearing such a boring wardrobe.

"Has anyone ever said no to you?" He didn't bother with a polite greeting.

"Not when something as important as my life is involved." She mentally thanked herself for Allie's forwardness. She sensed Brianne could never have handled someone as strong as Pete. But Allie could. And would. "So where are we going?"

He stared at her for a long moment. The look in his eyes was intimidating, but she didn't back down, instead gazing back with smiling innocence.

The tiniest of smiles touched his own lips. "You up to some dinner?"

"Is that an invitation?"

"Best you'll get from me." He gestured for her to precede him. "It's down the block. You willing to walk?"

"Best form of exercise around." She waited until he reached her side. "Have you learned anything yet?"

He slanted her a look that gave away nothing of his thoughts. "Other than you having a fight with your fiancé?"

"We didn't have a fight." She had a feeling she was lying, but refused to back down.

"It was more than a disagreement and less than a knock-down drag-out," he stated. "A lot of witnesses will back up the statement, too. It was a real bad idea to have your battle in public. I didn't think the rich did such things."

She waved a hand dismissively. "One person's opinion."

"Not according to the cops. They're having a great time listening to your so-called close friends tell all about you. The way I hear it, some stories are perfect tabloid material." He jammed his hands in his jeans pockets as they walked along. He hadn't made any allowances for her smaller stature by shortening his stride and privately admitted he was surprised she was keeping up. For a woman he thought of as a cream puff she was showing a bit of steel in her spine. Not that he was going to admit it, mind you. But by now, he figured she would have dissolved in a flood of tears, indulging in a good crying bout in an attempt to solicit his sympathy. Either she sensed tears wouldn't do her any good or she wasn't the kind to break down easily. He knew he'd find out more about her the moment she discovered their destination. If she was the snob he figured her to be, she would refuse to step inside. And it would be easier to kiss her off.

"They're talking to everyone but me!"

"Probably because they already have a good idea what you're going to say." Pete used the flat of his palm to push open the glass door, stepping back to allow Brianne to pass him. He was surprised by the expression on her face as she stopped short and looked around. There was no disgust or revulsion. Only something that he swore looked like sorrow.

Brianne knew where she was the moment she stepped in. After all, it was Wednesday, and every Wednesday Charlie cooked up his famous five-alarm chili. The pungent aroma of spices and meat permeated the room, causing a tickling sensation in the back of her throat. But it was the sudden sting in her eyes she felt most.

It had only been a matter of days, so she shouldn't have expected any changes. Since this was the shift she usually worked, it was natural another waitress would be waiting on her tables. She just didn't expect it to be someone she knew. She made a concerted effort not to greet the woman, who looked up and smiled and waved at Pete. Brianne also tried not to notice his hand resting against the small of her waist as he guided her toward one of the rear booths.

"Hi, Lil," he said, greeting the waitress.

"Coffee for both of you?" She looked at Brianne curiously, then warily, as comprehension set in.

"Please," Brianne said hoarsely.

Pete sat across from her with his hands resting on the tabletop. "I guess my choice of dining establishments isn't up to your standards."

"You have no idea what my standards are."

He inclined his head in acknowledgment. "No, but it's easy to guess. That outfit you're wearing probably cost more than Lil makes in a month."

She successfully hid her smile as she thought of confiding that she knew exactly what Lil made on a monthly basis. While the base pay wasn't the best, tips for the shapely waitress were well above average.

"Here you go." The woman in question slid coffee cups in front of each of them. "Know what you're going to have?"

"Charlie's chili," Pete said without hesitation.

"Since I'm not a glutton for heartburn, I'll take the BLT," Brianne told Lil.

"Charlie believes his chili isn't any good unless you get heartburn from it." The woman chuckled before moving off.

Brianne felt as if her smile was pasted on her lips. How many times had she said the exact same thing to customers, then sashayed back to the counter? She remembered even offering antacid pills to those unwary of Charlie's fiery concoctions. It wasn't until she looked at Pete and saw the concern etched on his features that she realized he had asked her something.

"I'm sorry, what did you say?"

"I asked if you were all right."

"My fiancé is dead, supposedly by my own hand. After all, I was found holding the murder weapon. Yet I honestly have no recollection of what happened, and I have a lawyer who's convinced I did it, but because of my family he's willing to do his part in making sure my sentence won't be too harsh for my tender sensibilities. What do you think?" she countered.

"At least the judge didn't ask for your passport."

She shot him a wry look. "Yes, he did. I wanted to tell him I had no desire to use a passport with such a horrible picture in it."

Pete's eyes crinkled at the corners as his laughter spilled out. Brianne felt a funny catch in the pit of her stomach as she stared at him. Allie had heard Pete laugh many times, but she hadn't ever felt like this. There hadn't been this sensation of falling into space as she heard the low, rumbling sound.

"Try and keep your sense of humor," he advised. "You're going to need it."

"You act as if you're surprised I even have one."

"I am. I figure people born with gold spoons in their mouths don't need a sense of humor."

"I never thought of myself as someone born with a gold spoon in her mouth," Brianne countered.

"Sorry," he said without a trace of apology, while amusement lightened his eyes. "I forgot how old the family fortune is. I guess it would be platinum, wouldn't it?"

"Damn straight."

His amusement fled as quickly as it appeared. "How can a woman have so many sides?" he murmured.

She was spared from answering when the waitress appeared with their meal. She set their plates down and made sure they didn't require anything else.

"Pete." Lil touched his arm. "We're holding the service for Allie tomorrow at two. Then we're all going to get together at my place to have a few drinks."

He nodded. A grim expression shadowed his features. "I'll be there."

Brianne shifted uneasily as she listened to them. Overhearing plans for her own funeral was proving to be more than a little unsettling. She picked up her sandwich, took a large bite and munched as if it was the most important thing in her life.

"Sorry," Pete murmured after Lil left them. "A waitress who worked here was killed recently."

"Oh, I'm sorry. " She fashioned her expression into a properly sympathetic one.

He nodded jerkily and looked down at his hands. "She was a good friend."

His quiet statement struck a chord deep in her heart.

Allie had always considered Pete a friend. If she had been honest with herself, she would have even admitted she had a bit of a crush on him. A crush she never would have acted on, because deep down she had never felt she was good enough for him. As a cop, Pete had been awarded citations for bravery and valor in duty. He was one of the most honest men she had ever known. He wouldn't even accept a free cup of coffee. When he left the force and worked for his private investigator's license, she had done her best to throw business his way. If nothing else, it guaranteed she'd see him an average of once a day for meals. He'd always acted like a good-natured brother, offering advice. Now she only wished she had taken his advice about Whit. She might still have been alive today! Except Allie was well known for not having the best taste in men. With her luck, she would have only chosen someone worse.

"We need to discuss your case." Pete broke into her thoughts. He dipped his spoon into the steaming chili and lifted it to his lips.

She grimaced. "Aren't you afraid of getting indigestion?"

"Nah, only Charlie's meatloaf does that." He grinned. "Now, tell me about that night. What started the fight?"

"Fight?" she echoed.

The argument Michael started with Brianne because she wasn't willing to set a date for their wedding, the voice whispered in her ear. *She told him she didn't think it would be a good idea to get married so soon. He drank too much at the country-club dance and was too loud.*

"I told him I wanted to wait to set a date for our wedding," she said in a low voice. That sounded pretty reasonable to her. Wouldn't it be logical for her to have some pre-wedding jitters? She only hoped the voice was telling her the truth.

I never lie.

"And he didn't like it?"

Brianne nodded. "He started drinking at the club and said things he shouldn't."

"Such as?" he prompted.

Help! She found out she could scream just as well inside her head as she could out loud.

Honestly, Brianne, can't you do anything for yourself? He let everyone know you were putting him off and he inferred you had a lover. You can do something with those little tidbits, can't you?

She hoped she appeared embarrassed as well as sorrowful over the chain of events. She toyed with her glass, tracing the rim with her fingernail.

"When Michael drinks, he gets a little too loud," she murmured. "He couldn't understand that I felt it was best we wait. He refused to understand that it had to do with me, not him. He accused me of having a lover," she added in a low voice.

Pete didn't take his eyes off her. "Do you?"

She had an instantaneous recollection of Whit sneering at Allie, his knife flashing as they struggled and the fire in her chest that had led to blackness.

"No," she said with strong conviction.

"Then why would he think you did?"

"He was spouting off because he couldn't come up with any other reason," she argued heatedly. "He didn't want to think I might be breaking up with him, so he came up with the best reason he could. Something that would save face. My having a lover would make him out to be the wounded party."

Pete's gaze didn't waver. He couldn't put his finger on it, but he sensed Brianne wasn't telling him the entire story.

"Were you thinking of breaking up with him?"

A small thought echoed in her head. "Yes."

"So you fought about changing the wedding date."

"No, he ranted and raved and I walked away." With surprisingly steady hands, she lifted her sandwich. "I don't like scenes."

"For someone who doesn't like scenes, you sure came up with a hell of a one," he said dryly.

"Why would I shoot him if I wanted to break our engagement?" she asked calmly. "Why not just tell him it's over and go on from there? It's not as if my very existence hinged on him."

"Maybe he wanted the ring back and you said no," Pete quipped. He pulled a small notebook out of his jacket pocket and opened it. "By the way, I called your attorney's office to set up a meeting. He didn't seem too happy that you'd let your fingers do the walking in search of a private eye."

She lifted her chin in a manner that he already knew meant she wasn't about to be put off. "As I told you before, it's my life on the line, not Joshua's. He will deal with you whether he likes it or not. When are you meeting him?"

"Day after tomorrow at two."

She made a mental note. "Then I'll meet you at his office. He's been wanting to talk to me anyway about that night." *A night I have no knowledge of.*

"Do you always get your way?" Pete asked.

Something deep inside gave her the answer a microsecond before she said it out loud. "Not usually when it counts. Perhaps that's why I'm so adamant now."

Adamant, Allie? Where the hell did you pick up the fancy vocabulary? her old self asked. *You finished high school by the skin of your teeth. Remember how*

*everyone said the only reason you passed English class
was because Mr. Garibaldi liked your legs?*

She finished her sandwich and drink and slid her
plate to one side.

"He also worked at the store, didn't he?"

Brianne nodded, unsure what direction his questioning was taking. "He was in charge of our two
stores in the Valley," she clarified.

*My dear, you are doing beautifully. And here you
thought you couldn't pull it off.*

She wanted to smile at the complimentary voice in
her head, but resisted the urge.

Pete looked up when Lil stopped by to pick up
Brianne's plate and see if they needed anything else.
After learning they didn't, she left them alone again.

"I'd like the authority to go over there and talk to
the employees," he said, as he reached into his back
pocket and pulled out his wallet. "See if there's anything they might know."

Brianne nodded. "I'll make sure they give you their
full cooperation," she said quietly.

Pete leaned back and peered at her through narrowed eyes. "I don't think you did it, princess," he
murmured. "But whoever did knew what they were
doing, because proving you didn't is going to be hard
as hell unless you can remember more about that
night."

"I wish I could." At least she could be honest there.
"The doctor feels I suffered a major shock, and in an
attempt to persuade myself it really didn't happen, I
blocked out the entire episode. He said it's fairly
common with major trauma like that."

"Any chance of it coming back?"

Only if the real Brianne Sinclair happens to return, she thought to herself on a wry note.

"There're no hard-and-fast rules." She still remembered the doctor explaining it to her as he treated her for shock. And was grateful she had that to fall back on, since she had so little of anything else.

Pete waved to Lil and Charlie as they walked out of the restaurant.

"The service is at eleven," Lil called after him. He nodded to let her know he heard.

"It seems as if you were in your home away from home back there," Brianne commented casually as they walked down the sidewalk.

"To be honest, it's probably more my home than my apartment is. Cooking isn't one of my strong points, so it's safer to go there." Sorrow crossed his features briefly. "It's not the same without Allie, though."

"The waitress who was killed?" she prodded.

He nodded. "It sounds like a cliché, but she really did have a heart of gold. If she liked you, there wasn't anything she wouldn't do to help out, but if she didn't, heaven help you." He smiled as a memory intruded. "About a year ago, some guy was in there giving Lil a hard time. It seems his coffee was first too cold, then too hot, then his food wasn't cooked right, and he kept sending stuff back. He ran her butt off. Then he started spouting off that they couldn't even season food properly and made quite a few comments about what he considered was less-than-adequate service. Allie finally walked over, picked up the saltshaker, took off the top and dumped the whole container on his chicken-fried steak. While she emptied the pepper shaker on top of the salt, she told him she hoped there was enough seasoning on it now. Then she stood over him and made sure he ate it.''

"Sounds like an Amazon." All right, she was shamelessly fishing for compliments, but she figured it wouldn't hurt.

"No, she wasn't all that tall, although it wasn't easy to tell since she always wore high heels. I never could figure out how she could work an entire shift in those heels, but she said heels showed off her legs more and got her bigger tips.'' He continued smiling. ''I have to admit she was right.''

"At least you have good memories of her," she said softly.

"Yeah." His smile disappeared. "And I'll have one more as soon as I put away her son-of-a-bitch boyfriend for killing her.''

"Didn't the police arrest him for murder?" she probed. She wished she had looked at the newspaper for word about her death, but frankly, the idea of reading about it make her nauseous.

"They couldn't hold him when there was nothing to prove he had anything to do with it," Pete said grimly. "I figure he had a few of his dealer friends come by, work him over and steal some of his stuff. He used the story that he and Allie surprised a burglar and he was beaten up while she was somehow killed in the struggle. He sure didn't waste any time in mourning her. He's already got a new honey and is walking around, while Allie's…'' He stopped. ''Sorry, it's a sore point with me.''

"I don't blame you!" She couldn't tell him the real reason she was angry. Whit hadn't been arrested for her death? How she'd love to track him down and give him a taste of his own medicine! That bastard!

"Oh, I intend to get him," he told her with a grim smile. "He's not going to get away with it. I'll make sure of that." He came to a stop alongside Brianne's car.

She laid her hand on his arm, feeling the muscles tense under her touch. "I'm glad you're still willing to help me." As she looked up at him, a jolt of something hit her deep within. The flaring of his smoke-colored eyes told her he felt it, too.

"It won't be easy."

"Nothing is." She dipped her head and dug through her purse until she found her keys. She disarmed the car alarm. "I'll see you at Joshua's office day after tomorrow then."

"I'll also want to talk to your family," he added. "Your mother and brother and sister-in-law."

Brianne grimaced. "Better you than me."

"Meaning?"

She thought back to Olivia's entrance into the solarium. "Let's just say I live with the reincarnated spirit of Joan Crawford."

Chapter Five

Pete hated funerals. He considered them a barbaric custom where the living congregated to mourn the dead whether they had liked the deceased or not. He had no idea why funerals were even held, since the deceased wasn't around to appreciate all the irony. He always said he wanted his friends gathered around him while he was alive to enjoy it. Which is why he would have preferred to be anywhere rather than sitting on a hard chair in this flower-filled parlor with classical music playing in the background. He pulled at his tie, hating the constricted feeling around his throat. Only for Allie would he wear a shirt that had been ironed.

"What the hell is this?" he demanded in a low voice to Lil, who sat beside him. For once her usually teased hair was pulled back in a sedate knot at the back of her head, her makeup was minimal and her black dress almost covered her knees. If he hadn't offered to pick her up for the service, he wouldn't have known it was she. "None of this is Allie," he muttered, looking as if he couldn't breathe properly. Considering the tie and dress shirt, he didn't feel as if he could.

Lil looked shocked at his comment. "We're honoring her. That's why we're here."

"Honor, hell." He grimaced and pulled at his tie again as the minister asked if anyone would like to say a few words.

Pete didn't even stop to think. He got to his feet and gingerly climbed over Lil's legs. The moment he stepped up to the podium and looked at the people in front of him, he wondered if he had made a mistake. But before he could question himself any further, he dove right in with an impromptu speech.

"Allie would have hated this," he announced. He ignored the shocked murmurs traveling around the room. "She wasn't delicate flowers, classical music or black clothing. She was bright red lipstick, flashy colors, the Rolling Stones, and I happen to know she only drank tequila shooters. She was happiest when she was out dancing all night, then cussing us out at Charlie's during the day." He took a deep breath in an attempt to sort out his jumbled thoughts. "She was giving. I knew her for more than eight years, but while we talked a lot, I don't think I ever got to know all of her. She made sure leftovers were given to the homeless, she looked after all her friends one way or another." A tiny smile curved his lips. "But I'll be the first to admit she wasn't a saint."

"That's for damn sure!" one man said loudly. "Because she didn't feel I tipped her enough she used to add it on to my bill!"

"Good thing, Harry, since your idea of a tip is a nickel," Lil retorted, getting in the act. "When my son was sick with the flu, she worked my shift so Charlie wouldn't fire me."

With that, the ball was rolling, and many mourners brought up typical Allie moments they remembered.

Pete blinked rapidly. "Dammit, she was only thirty-one," he said hoarsely. "No one should die that young."

"No one should die because of that slimy SOB, Whit." Allie's former neighbor began sobbing into her handkerchief. "I don't care what anyone says. He was behind her death. I know he was!"

Pete bit back his own comments on the subject. He intended to nail Whit his own way. This was not the place to ask the woman if she knew anything. He'd stop by her apartment another day.

"You know the Irish have the right idea with a wake," he said. "They get together, get drunk and re-call old times. Why can't we let Allie go that way? The way she would have wanted?"

As if by unspoken consent, the mourners formed a line, passing by the casket with either a murmured word or fingertips pressed against the wood.

After Allie was interred, Pete and Lil were the last to leave the cemetery.

"I'm really going to miss her," she whispered as she settled in the passenger seat of Pete's car. "This new girl Charlie hired is all right, but she isn't Allie."

"No, there isn't another Allie." His foot faltered on the accelerator as a picture came to mind: Brianne Sinclair with flashing eyes and pert words.

Funny, with all the research he'd done on the woman so far, he hadn't picked up any hint of this side of her. She was considered quiet and reserved. Dressed conservatively and didn't believe in making a ripple. She had a position with the family stores, but wasn't known to spend a lot of time there, nor was she missed by co-workers. So why, while he was thinking of Allie, would Brianne come to mind? It didn't make sense, but then he was discovering that lately not too much was making sense.

She's only a client, he reminded himself. *Someone like her isn't for the likes of you.*

BRIANNE DIDN'T ENJOY the day. Not when she knew that on the other side of town a funeral was being held for her. It was an unsettling thought, and by rights she shouldn't have continued thinking about it. But forgetting wasn't easy.

"I hope no one wore black or played boring music. Funerals seem to have the most mundane music," she murmured to herself as she surveyed the contents of her closet. "This woman has more clothes than a department store, so why can't I find something to wear?" She plucked out a cream-colored, raw-silk suit and gazed at it with dislike. "She has very boring taste." She moved past the suits, past dresses and on to more casual clothing, still dressier than anything she had ever worn.

Do not use the third person when referring to yourself.

"No one is around," she said softly. "And it's not easy to think of Brianne as me when I look at all these very boring clothes."

Why should you worry about something you can change?

"What am I supposed to change?" She pulled out yet another pair of oatmeal-colored raw-silk pants. "How many pairs could one person own in the same color?'' She put them back in the closet. "There isn't one bright-colored garment in here.''

Brianne wasn't into bright colors. She believed she gave the world a more serene image if she remained true to neutral tones. I think, in her own way, she was trying to hide.

"Well, something has to be done about this.'' She pulled open drawer after drawer, revealing delicate lingerie, all in shades ranging from snowy white to candlelight to a creamy pearl. "Her underwear is gorgeous but boring! I can't live with this wardrobe. I have to have color in my life.''

And you have the charge accounts to purchase that color if that's what you feel you need. Didn't you mention you were going to stop by the store this morning? Do some shopping then.

"I'm not sure that's a good suggestion,'' Brianne said, suddenly feeling uneasy at the idea of spending money that wasn't by rights hers.

You are now Brianne Sinclair. What is hers is now yours. Do with it what you feel best.

"The family will probably think I'm a few minus a six-pack.''

You've had a shock. You want to embrace life again and this is your way of doing just that.

"Well, if you put it that way.'' She considered the suggestion. "I have charge cards, a checkbook and the family owns a chain of department stores. Brianne deserves a little vitality in her life, and it looks like it's up to me to give it to her.'' Humming under her breath, she danced over to the stereo system and turned on the radio. She grimaced as the soft soothing sounds of Mozart filtered out of the speakers spread around the room. "No way." She spun the dial until she found the oldies rock station she favored. She turned up the volume as Credence Clearwater blared out of the speakers. "Much better!"

Brianne quickly dressed in a black skirt and chose a white blouse, which she left unbuttoned at the collar. After sorting through the large jewelry chest that held costume pieces, each one still more valuable than anything she had ever owned, she settled on a delicate cameo fastened to a black-velvet ribbon. She mumbled her dissatisfaction regarding the makeup choices and lipsticks and quickly transferred her possessions from one purse to another. As she gazed at the gold key ring with a fancy medallion on the end she thought of the whimsical, glitter-dusted-fairy key ring Pete had given her for her last birthday. She knew it hadn't cost much, but the gift had touched her. Whit had gotten drunk that evening and stayed out all night.

"I went from Whit to a dead fiancé," she murmured, heading for the stairs. "Too bad it wasn't the other way around."

"What are you doing?" Trey, wearing an impeccably cut, charcoal, lightweight wool suit, walked out into the hallway as she headed for the front door.

She didn't pause in her stride. "I'm going to the store."

He frowned and reached out to detain her. "What about breakfast?"

"I'll get something on the way."

"Brianne, I don't think that would be a good idea."

She kept her hand on the knob as she looked over her shoulder. "It's not a good idea to pick up some breakfast on the way? They all say breakfast is the most important meal of the day.''

Trey still frowned, obviously not understanding the new Brianne's form of humor. ''Bri, it's not a good idea for you to go to the store,'' he flatly stated.

She turned around fully. ''Why not?''

He shifted from one foot to the other. ''Well, you haven't been acting like yourself lately. And now this...'' He waved a hand in her direction.

She was rapidly losing her patience with this man. Even if he happened to be her brother. ''What?''

''You're under suspicion for murder and some people at the store might feel uncomfortable seeing you walking around free. Michael was very well liked by all the personnel.''

Do you wonder why he is lying?

Brianne had to wonder just that. If there was one thing Allie could sniff out, it was a liar. She didn't need to sniff hard when it came to Trey. He was a horrible liar. She supposed she would just have to show him how it should be done.

''The last few days have been very hard for me, Trey,'' she said softly, mentally appealing to his gentler side. ''I can't just hide away here in the house. If I do, I will look guilty to people, because they will think I don't want to face anyone. By going to the store, I can show them I feel comfortable enough to be among them because I am innocent.'' She faced him squarely, forcing him to look at her. ''I need to make some changes within myself. And the best place to start is at the store.''

His smile might have been reassuring, but the skepticism in his eyes told her another story.

"Good luck."

"Now what did he mean by that?" she murmured, walking out to her car.

You'll find out soon enough.

Brianne rolled her eyes. "No hint?"

No, I believe this is something you should find out for yourself.

SINCLAIR'S FIRST STORE had been located on the same corner in Beverly Hills for the last fifty years, which pretty much made it an institution for many serious shoppers. It was three stories, with cosmetics, jewelry, women's sportswear, men's clothing and the shoe salon on the ground floor; lingerie, women's dresses, fur salon, formal wear, restaurant and beauty salon on the second floor. The third was taken up with administrative offices.

Thanks to her mentor's prompting, Brianne easily found her personal parking spot and the rear door. She greeted the security guard by name and headed for the elevator. There was no mistaking the surprise etched on his face at seeing her.

Blessedly alone in the elevator, she took a deep breath as she watched the numbers slowly change.

"You deal with marketing," she murmured. "Go in, say hello to your secretary, see if there's anything important they need signed, then say you want to walk through the store."

Brianne drew upon Allie's bravado as she walked down the lushly carpeted hallway. She smiled and nodded at people she passed and noted the various expressions crossing their faces. None of them were comforting.

"Ms. Sinclair." A woman in her late twenties looked up from her typing. Even she didn't look welcoming. "I'm surprised you're here. Ah, con-considering what's happened," she stammered.

Brianne raised her hand to halt her explanation. "I saw no reason to stay in the house when there's work to be done, Gwen."

The secretary was hot on her heels as she walked into her office. The young woman was so discomfited at seeing her boss that she didn't notice her looking around the room as if she had never seen it before. Brianne settled herself in her chair. By now, she wasn't surprised to find the decor done in pale cream and peach with a touch of pearl gray. She wondered if the real Brianne had ever thought of adding a dash of red or purple to her life. Maybe she wouldn't have been so uptight if she had.

"I'll get your coffee for you," Gwen murmured.

"Don't worry about that," she answered. "I thought I'd walk through the store, do a little shopping." She stared at her empty In box. "Is there anything I need to look at?"

"Of course not!" Gwen blushed, then forged ahead. "No, not just now."

Brianne ran her hand across the desktop. Dust free. "Well then," she said brightly, "I think I'll look around the store and pick up a few things."

"Ms. Sinclair, are you all right?" Gwen ventured.

She kept her smile pasted on her lips. "Fine."

Brianne forced herself to walk slowly down the hallway to the elevator. She first stopped in the dress department. Two women immediately approached her.

"Ms. Sinclair." One inclined her head in greeting and smiled, while the other watched her warily. "It's nice to see you again. We just received a new shipment from your favorite designer. Let me show you a few things I put aside for you."

"One minute, Sarah." She placed her hand on the woman's arm. "Are they the same color I usually buy?"

The salesclerk nodded, confused by her question.

"I would honestly prefer seeing something with more color." She spied a dress on a mannequin and headed in that direction. "Such as this." She held up the filmy skirt to a cobalt blue dress. "I want to look at clothes that have some life in them."

The woman was wide-eyed with shock. "Bright colors?" she whispered. "But Ms. Sinclair, you never wear bright colors. You've always felt they didn't suit you."

"Then it's time I do something about it," she said as she wandered through the department.

Within minutes, word had spread through the store like wildfire. There was something very wrong with Ms. Sinclair. She smiled openly, was friendly, and even more shocking was the fact that not one item she bought was beige, cream, pale pink or off white! She cut a wide swathe through the dress department, worked her way through lingerie and then down to jewelry, shoes and cosmetics. Even her usual muted rose or peach lipsticks were disdained in favor of dusky roses and bright corals. No two-inch heels on pumps for her, not as long as she could find high heels to go with her new wardrobe. Everything was boxed up to be delivered to her home.

"Hair next," she decided, stopping by the beauty salon.

"Ms. Sinclair." The manager greeted her with a toothy smile that bordered on the curious. Word about her strange behavior had already reached her. "How can we help you?"

"Something needs to be done to my hair," she declared.

The woman warily eyed the elegant French twist Brianne wore. "But you just had it trimmed a week ago."

"No, I want something new." She thought for a moment. "What about a perm?"

"A perm?"

She nodded. "I'd really like to have some curl."

Don't you feel you're overdoing it?

You're the one who suggested I could do this, she answered silently, watching the manager scurry inside and gesture wildly to one of the hairdressers. Her heart sank when the two women walked back out.

"Ms. Sinclair, I understand you'd like a perm," the second woman said with a stiff smile.

Rosalie, your usual hairdresser, isn't happy with your request.

"I need a change, Rosalie."

"But the way you wear your hair is perfect for your facial symmetry," she protested.

"There's always more than one way for a person to wear her hair." Brianne looked past her toward one of the women in the salon. The way her hair swung in loose curls told her this woman would know what she was looking for. "Isn't she new here?" She nodded toward the woman. After the manager confirmed the fact, Brianne said, "Then I'd like to try her if she has the time."

Becca, the new hairdresser, looked at her with a wariness Brianne was rapidly recognizing.

"You want me to do your hair?"

"That's right, and I want something new," she explained, picking up a hairstylist magazine and thumbing through it. One style caught her eye and she held it up. "Such as this."

Becca stepped forward and pulled the pins out of Brianne's hair. She combed her fingers through the strands and pulled them forward. She cocked her head one way, then another as she studied Brianne's face and the texture of her hair. She suddenly smiled. "I can't wait to see the results." She practically pulled Brianne to the dressing room and handed her a smock.

As Becca shampooed, conditioned, trimmed and rolled her hair, Brianne imagined she could hear the excited buzz of conversation throughout the store again.

I'm sure they all think I've lost my marbles or I'm having a makeover for my new man—one everybody thinks I already have, she thought to herself as she sat back and relaxed under Becca's knowing hands.

It wasn't any wonder that the idea of a new man in her life brought Pete's face to mind.

The trouble was, thinking about him reminded her what he was doing today. He was attending Allie's funeral. *Her* funeral. She shifted uneasily in the chair as her stomach lurched in a threatening manner.

"Ms. Sinclair, are you all right?" Becca asked, her hands hovering over Brianne's head.

"Fine." She flashed her a reassuring smile. "I just happened to think of something." *Such as wondering who all showed up for my funeral. I hope Charlie sent flowers. It's the least he could do. And I hope Pete didn't let Whit attend. That weasel. I hope he doesn't think he can get away with my murder. Because after Pete helps me find out who killed Michael, I want him to pin Whit to the wall. With real nails.* She began smiling as she visualized him literally nailed to the wall.

When Becca began combing out Brianne's hair, she turned her chair away from the mirror. "I want you to be surprised with what I've done," she explained, for the first time looking a little uneasy.

Brianne sensed the younger woman's nervousness was because this was so different from her usual style. She already knew she had made the right choice.

Now that she was facing the room, Brianne noticed the furtive whispers happening among the patrons and the looks directed her way. Many of them were laced with suspicion. As both customers and staff noticed her gaze, they hurriedly picked up a magazine or none-too-subtly turned back to one another. Brianne wouldn't have been surprised if every item of clothing she'd purchased was being discussed at great length.

Old biddies, she thought to herself, presenting all of them with a dazzling smile. *They're probably shocked that I'm daring to show my face in public after the tragedy. Oh yes, that has to be the word they're using.*

"Close your eyes, Ms. Sinclair," Becca suggested, slowly turning the chair around. Her fingers combed through Brianne's hair, fluffing it. "All right, you can open them now."

Brianne slowly opened her eyes and just sat there for a moment, savoring the changes. Instead of smoothed back into an intricate twist or braid, her hair had been trimmed and shaped, with a perm adding wave to the ash blond tresses. She noticed the style added a piquancy to her features. Thanks to the brighter-colored lipstick and eye makeup, she no longer looked as if she could easily blend in with the furniture. And if she looked closely, she could swear she saw a trace of the old Allie deep in her eyes.

Panic suddenly swept over her. *What am I doing?* she mentally screamed at herself. *I'm not some jet-set socialite with a fancy education. I only finished high school because my mother threatened to whip my butt but good if I didn't.*

Easy there. If you have an anxiety attack right now, they're going to think you're guilty, and your actions will be duly reported to whomever will listen. Now take a deep breath, smile and compliment Becca on her lovely work.

For once, the voice was comforting. Brianne managed to dredge up a smile and turn to Becca.

"This is exactly what I wanted," she said sincerely and honestly.

The hairdresser's face lit up with joy. "Thank you, Ms. Sinclair," she said softly.

Brianne pushed herself to her feet with the intention of walking to the dressing room to change out of the smock. She stopped and turned back to Becca. "I hope you'll have time for me again."

She went into the dressing room, changed out of the smock and back into her skirt and blouse. She thought longingly of the clothing she'd purchased that morning and wished she had kept one outfit to wear. She was grateful the new makeup colors and hairstyle jazzed up what would otherwise be a dull-looking outfit.

"Brianne, you're worrying too much," she told her reflection in the mirror. "You're not supposed to do that anymore, remember? You are a woman in charge of your life. Such as it is." She adjusted the cameo necklace and walked out.

Brianne tipped Becca and signed the charge slip for services before stopping off at the restaurant. Several women nodded and smiled at her, and thanks to the voice in her head, she was able to respond with the proper name each time.

"Such a tragedy," one silk-clad matron confided, giving Brianne an airy kiss against both cheeks. Her eyes were avid with the prospect of hearing something juicy she could pass on to friends.

Brianne wondered if the real Ms. Sinclair knew what kind of barracudas claimed to be her friends. Judging from the little she'd overheard so far, she had never been viewed as a bitch or vicious toward another. So why would people think she'd shot Michael? she asked herself later as she went upstairs to her office.

Gwen looked up from her typing as she came in. "Shipping called and said your packages will be delivered this afternoon, Ms. Sinclair," she said in her soft voice. The look she sneaked at her employer was wary at best. "Your hair looks very nice."

"Thank you." Brianne eyed her. "You can't tell me that's all you heard since I've been gone."

The young woman blushed furiously. Her fingers seemed to stumble over the computer keys. She finally lifted them off the keyboard. "You haven't had any other calls."

Some of Allie's cockiness showed as Brianne stood there with one shapely hip thrust out, a hand jammed on it. "Oh come on, Gwen. The gossip about me must have been good. Did they start with a detailed description of the clothes I bought? What are they saying? That the esteemed Brianne Sinclair has finally lost it?" she pressed. "All of a sudden she's having her hair permed. She bought all these new clothes in bright colors and, hot damn, she even bought a bright red lipstick!"

Gwen shook her head. Her eyes were wide. "No one said anything bad about you."

Brianne took pity on her. "Gwen, this past week has been a very difficult time for me," she said slowly. "I haven't been feeling like my old self lately and I thought coming in to the store and throwing myself into my work would help. The shopping trip was another way of my handling stress. I hope you'll help me get back on track. Now what's next for us? Is there anything important that should be handled before the end of the day?"

"But you don't do anything here!" the woman blurted out. Then she gasped and covered her mouth with her hands. "I'm sorry!"

Brianne grew still. "What you're saying is that my name might be on the office door, but my brother makes sure I keep my fingers out of the business."

Gwen's head bobbed up and down. She watched her boss with dazed fascination. "You always said you never minded," she whispered.

Her smile wasn't the least bit pleasant. "That was before. But since then I've been considered off my rocker. I'm doing strange things and it's only natural that I keep up the reputation of being unstable by doing something very unusual here." She paused. "Let's shock the hell out of everyone."

"How?" Gwen asked in a hoarse whisper.

"Easy. I'll actually do some work."

"WHAT THE HELL DO YOU think you're doing?" Trey pounced on Brianne the moment he arrived home that evening.

She didn't blink at his tone. "I went into the store, did a little shopping, had my hair done, ate a lovely lunch in the restaurant and went over some paperwork with my secretary." She ticked each item off on her fingers.

"Did a *little* shopping?" He looked as if he was ready to pull his hair out by the roots. "Do you realize how much you spent?"

"To the penny. I have all the receipts. Honestly, Trey, are you depriving me of a proper wardrobe?"

"You have a perfectly adequate wardrobe. You were voted one of the best-dressed women in town last year," he retorted.

"In my opinion it should have been most-boringly dressed," she argued. "Trey, I cannot wear colorless clothing anymore."

He took a deep breath. "And that's why you sent me that memo?"

"I sent you a memo because I want to do something worthwhile at the store."

"You are a lucky woman to even be allowed to have an office there."

Brianne and Trey turned at the sound of the voice coming from the stairs. Olivia had just exited from the elevator. She was dressed in a simple black gown with a silver chain around her neck. A rare black pearl was embedded in what looked like a chunk of silver. Black pearl earrings adorned her ears.

Aren't you lucky? Your mother is going to dine with the family tonight. Better you than me.

Thanks a lot, Brianne said mentally.

Olivia looked up at her and Brianne tensed, afraid the older woman would again insist she wasn't her daughter. Olivia's green eyes surveyed her with alarming thoroughness.

"So you spent a small fortune at the store, did you?" A slight moue of distaste touched her lips as she studied her tousled hairstyle and the bright turquoise linen sheath that ended several inches above the knee. Her high heels matched her dress. "Obviously, Sinclairs is catering to an entirely different clientele these days. I'm not sure I approve."

"I think it's very becoming." Brianne brushed an imaginary bit of lint from her dress. "I needed something bright and cheerful."

"I'd like to remind you that your fiancé will be buried day after tomorrow. I don't think that outfit is appropriate mourning attire."

"I have a black suit for that." She only wished she knew what Brianne really thought of Michael.

"I understand you will be meeting with Joshua tomorrow," Olivia continued.

Brianne nodded. "Yes, at two."

Olivia turned to Trey. "Cancel any appointments you have tomorrow afternoon. We will need to go with Brianne to show our support."

"No." She quickly backpedaled. "What I mean is, you don't need to come along. We're only going to discuss strategy."

Olivia's expression didn't change, but something in her eyes told Brianne her protest was noted and ignored.

"Naturally, we'll be there. I want to make sure Joshua handles this correctly."

Brianne thought about telling her mother that Pete would be present at the meeting, too, then dismissed the thought. No, she'd let him handle Olivia. Knowing Pete, she figured he could probably handle her better than Brianne ever could. The fact that she felt a tiny tickle of awareness deep in her tummy at the thought of seeing Pete again was ignored. After all, she was no longer his buddy Allie. And while she knew he was interested in Brianne, she doubted he would do anything about it.

But I won't sock him one if he makes a pass, she mused to herself, smothering her smile before Olivia noticed it and commented on it. There was no way she was about to explain that thought!

Chapter Six

"Surely you do not intend to go to Joshua's office wearing *that?*"

At the sound of her mother's voice, Brianne looked down at her dress. Stopping several inches above the knee, the hot pink cotton dress had bands of bright turquoise and brilliant yellow around the short sleeves. She wore a multistrand beaded necklace in the same bright colors to accent the V neck, and she couldn't help but admire the turquoise high heels. Allie had always loved clothes and bright colors, and it was that part of her that had chosen new clothing the day before. Brianne had already sorted through the old wardrobe and piled most of it on the bed with the intention of giving it to charity.

Olivia, dressed in a severely cut dark purple suit with pearls, locked eyes with her daughter.

"Brianne would never wear such a vivid color," she said in a low voice that literally throbbed with meaning.

"My life has taken some very strange turns lately." Brianne spoke carefully, feeling as if she was sitting on a powder keg. "I've thought about it long and hard, and I've decided life's too short to worry about how people perceive me as a person, about the way I dress and act. I can't live the way you want me to any longer. I need to find out who I really am."

"Who you really are is not my daughter. That is obvious."

"Honestly, Mother, are you going on about that again?" Trey, looking irritated, walked into the dining room. The moment he seated himself at the long mahogany table, a cup of coffee and a plate holding salad was placed in front of him. "Maybe you should talk to the doctor about that new medication he has you on."

Olivia turned her steely gaze on him. "And perhaps you should stop and think what all of this is doing to the family name and leave any mention of medication I am on to my doctor and myself."

He looked up from his copy of the *Wall Street Journal,* which he hadn't had time to read that morning. It looked as if he wasn't going to be allowed to read it now, either. "She didn't mean to kill him. I'm sure Joshua will advise us how to handle the situation and control any damage."

Brianne rolled her eyes. "Oh, for heaven's sake, we're not talking about a parking ticket here!" she snapped, turning on her brother. "For the record, I didn't kill Michael. And I'd like to remind you I didn't deliberately run out to do something to besmirch the family name."

His lips twisted. "Good try, Bri, but it won't work. Don't forget I was the one who found you standing over the body with the gun in your hand. And all you can say is you have no idea what happened!"

"Because I don't!"

"Children, remember the servants." Olivia's quietly spoken reminder was an effective deterrent. She sipped her tea with her usual calm manner. "Arguments will only ruin the digestion. I suggest we drop this discussion until later. Trey, did you make sure Walter will have the car out front for us?"

"I'll be driving myself." Brianne broke the news.

"You will not," Olivia countered. "We will be showing a united front by driving there together."

"To be honest, I don't even know why you're going. It's my problem."

The older woman set her teacup down with casual disdain for the rare china. "It's your problem because you were foolish enough to align yourself with Michael in the beginning. Now the problem embodies the Sinclair name because it is on trial just as much as you are. I intend to let as little dirt as possible cling to it."

What a lovely woman you have for a mother, Brianne. Do you suppose she pulls wings off butterflies for fun?

Brianne hadn't taken her eyes from her mother. *I bet she deliberately messes up her bathroom just because she feels the upstairs maid doesn't have enough to do,* she thought to herself. "I would prefer to drive myself, since I have errands to run," she returned calmly. She thought about dropping her second bombshell about Pete, then changed her mind. No, she'd wait until the two met.

"Then you will change before the meeting." Olivia made it an order, not a suggestion.

Brianne stood up. "No, I don't think so. This color cheers me up, and right now I need all the cheering up I can get. Now if you'll excuse me, I have a few things to do before the meeting. I'll see you at Joshua's office."

She kept her back ramrod straight as she climbed the stairs. "I bet she refuses to tip waitresses because she figures they earn enough," she muttered to herself once she was in her room. She looked at the serene surroundings and promptly dropped into a chair. She was finding out that sparring with her mother took a lot of energy. "I've got to get out of here full-time. Why didn't she find herself an apartment so she would be away from that witch?"

Because Olivia thoroughly intimidated Brianne, her voice told her. *Brianne decided it was easier to stay here than risk a battle with her mother on the issue of moving out.*

"Well, too bad, because I intend to find my own place."

You realize that if you can't unmask the real killer your "own place" will be a prison cell.

Brianne looked up at the ceiling. "Thank you so much for that inspiring piece of news!" She pushed herself out of her chair. "I guess it's too much to hope that Pete learned something already."

Would you care for me to tell you about your funeral.

She swallowed, feeling the nausea crawl up her throat at the idea. "I don't think so."

It was a lovely service.

"Great. I'm glad to hear it, but I don't want to hear about it!" She gritted her teeth.

Peter said some very complimentary things about you, although, after dealing with you these past few days, I'm sure he had to have greatly exaggerated.

Brianne closed her eyes. "I said I don't want to hear about it." She pronounced each word with deadly intent, then headed for the bathroom and hastily reapplied her lipstick. She stepped back and studied the final result. No more insipid pinks for this woman, no sirree!

"Why she never made use of her coloring I'll never know." She dropped the lipstick into her purse. "No wait, let me guess. Mom had something to do with her wardrobe, too. I'll tell you, if Brianne Sinclair was going to kill anyone in this house, it wouldn't have been Michael. It would have been her mother!"

BRIANNE GLORIED IN HER brief victory at driving herself to the attorney's office, although for a moment she feared her mother would insist on going with her. Luckily, Olivia didn't feel safe in anything smaller than a limousine. Brianne was positive she spent the drive giving Trey another long list of instructions. It appeared she was notorious for ruling everyone's life.

"No wonder her daughter couldn't handle anything," Brianne muttered to herself, as she pulled into the underground parking garage adjacent to the office building. "The family wouldn't let her."

That's why you're here.

"You said I was here to make things right," she reminded the voice. Then she asked again suddenly, "Are you sure you don't have a name I can call you?"

It hasn't been used in many centuries.

"Centuries, huh? How old are you?" She spied an empty parking slot and slid into it.

Old enough.

"That really tells me a lot. Are you allowed to reveal your name? Or is that against some cosmic rule?"

I was called Mathias.

"Can I call you Matt?"

If you feel the need to call me something it will have to be Mathias. In all my years of doing this, I have never dealt with anyone like you, Brianne.

"Yeah, I am one of a kind," she said proudly, stepping out of the BMW. She set the car alarm and walked briskly toward the elevator. Thanks to her internal guide, she knew enough to punch the button for the thirtieth floor. When the elevator arrived at the appropriate level she stepped off and walked down the carpeted hallway to the end office. She pushed open one of the double doors and entered the reception area, where her heels immediately sank into plush, pearl gray carpeting. Not looking right or left, Brianne walked toward an elegant piece of furniture reminiscent of an old English writing desk. An equally elegant woman was seated behind it. Her smile managed to be welcoming, yet at the same time not stretch any facial muscles.

"Ms. Sinclair, your mother and brother are already in with Mr. Randolph," the woman told her in a breathy voice. Her gaze, wary at best, drifted past Brianne. "A gentleman is also here, claiming to be an investigator you hired." Her doubtful tone indicated she couldn't believe Brianne would employ such a person.

Brianne turned around to find Pete lounging on a sofa better suited for a drawing room than a law office.

"Yes, I did hire Mr. Hackett." She continued staring at Pete. "Is there any reason why you're out here rather than in Mr. Randolph's office?" she asked him.

He stood up with his usual lazy grace. Dressed in his jeans, wrinkled tan shirt and battered leather jacket, he looked like a mutt who had happened to wander into the Westminster Dog Show. His one concession to the formal surroundings was a tie hanging loosely around his neck, as if he'd thrown it on in a hurry.

"Randolph's guardian of the holy portal wouldn't let me go in until you gave your approval," he explained. He looked at her slowly from head to toes. When he lifted his gaze back to her face, there was something new in his eyes—a very strong appreciation of what he saw. "Nice threads."

"Thanks. I thought I needed a new image."

"Good idea. The nun look has been out-of-date for quite some time now."

Brianne could have stood there and feasted her eyes on Pete for much longer if it wasn't for their interested audience.

"I'll take Mr. Hackett back with me, Carolyn," she told the receptionist.

The young woman nodded. As they passed, Brianne couldn't help noticing the interest in her eyes. Carolyn might not think Pete belonged in the hallowed offices of Randolph, Randolph and Greggs, but she obviously thought that didn't mean he wouldn't belong in another setting. Preferably something more intimate. Like her bedroom.

Clean up your mind, she ordered herself as she walked down the hallway. *You've known this man too long to think he'd want anything to do with a cold fish like her.*

Pete was fast on her heels, admiring the view from behind. He'd had no idea the woman had such great legs! Before, he'd sensed something hidden deep within her. The bright color of her dress seemed to highlight that hidden part of her—a part he decided he wouldn't mind getting to know better. He had an idea there was a lot about Brianne Sinclair most people didn't know.

Brianne stopped at the end office and knocked softly before opening the door and stepping inside, looking over her shoulder to make sure Pete was following. Warm-colored wood paneling did nothing to warm the room's atmosphere. The furniture was expensive and antique. Obviously, Joshua wanted his well-heeled clients to know he would give them their money's worth.

"Good afternoon," she said, greeting the occupants.

"Brianne." Joshua Randolph gave her a warm smile that dimmed when he noticed the man behind her. "Is there a problem?"

"Nothing more than that your receptionist wouldn't allow Mr. Hackett back here," she said breezily, taking the chair offered her. She gave the older man a pointed look until he gestured for Pete to be seated. Pete pulled the chair over to Brianne's side and seated himself. "Mr. Hackett is the private investigator I hired."

Olivia glanced at Pete as if he was something disagreeable the cat had dragged in. "If you wished to hire someone, you should have sought Joshua's advice on the matter, Brianne. I'm sure he would have found you someone appropriate."

There was that word again, Brianne thought. Why was it so important to them?

"As Joshua doesn't have any practical knowledge of criminal law, I decided I'd be better off looking for someone on my own. Mr. Hackett is well versed on the subject, as he used to be a highly decorated homicide detective."

Trey grimaced. "As if you know anything about it," he muttered, then looked away when his mother glared at him.

"We were just discussing your case," Olivia continued, as if neither had spoken. "And how it should be handled."

Brianne felt a sense of foreboding. "Oh, really? And what have you decided?" She leaned back in her chair, crossing her legs at the knee and looking as unconcerned as if they were discussing nothing more important than the weather. She couldn't help but notice that Pete's eyes were riveted on her legs. When he looked up he merely grinned, obviously not the least bit guilty about getting caught. She smiled back.

"I feel the best way to handle things is to plead diminished capacity," Joshua intoned. He glanced at Pete. "Naturally, with such a strong defense, we will not require Mr. Hackett's assistance."

Brianne felt a chill deep within her body. "Diminished capacity," she repeated. "What you really mean is you're going to tell them I'm nuts."

Olivia winced at the word. "Obviously, we would hope for something else, but Joshua feels that will work best, considering everything. After all, you and Michael were having problems. He might have provoked you to act as you did."

Brianne ignored her mother as she kept her gaze on the attorney. "Which means?"

He looked uncomfortable. "Naturally, the court will ask for a doctor's opinion, so you will need to speak to someone the court would approve of. Also, a short stay in an appropriate facility might be required."

"What you're talking about is a psych ward!" Brianne pushed herself out of her chair. "Are you all crazy?" She suddenly laughed at what she'd just asked. "Wait a minute, you're saying I'm the crazy one. I suddenly went off my rocker and shot Michael. Well, that makes a hell of a lot of sense."

"I don't appreciate that language!" Olivia's voice cracked like a whip.

"And I don't appreciate the accusation that I'm nuts!" Brianne turned on her mother.

"There's no other way this can be handled," Trey interjected.

"I didn't kill Michael," Brianne insisted. The expressions of the three told her they didn't believe her. Only Pete's face, kept carefully neutral, gave her hope. "I had no reason to kill him. Therefore, what we should be doing is finding out who really killed him."

"Don't even try that tactic, Bri," Trey muttered. "Everyone knew you two weren't getting along."

She searched deep within her soul and instinctively sensed that the real Brianne Sinclair hadn't killed her fiancé.

She shook her head. "Then I guess there's only one thing to do. And that's find an attorney who will believe in me and not listen to what my mother says." She picked up her purse and glanced at Pete. He obligingly got to his feet.

"Brianne, you will listen to Joshua's advice," Olivia ordered.

She walked to the door. "I'm not listening to anyone but a criminal attorney. Sorry to have wasted your time, Joshua."

"Brianne, you will come back in here," Olivia commanded as she opened the door and stepped out.

"Trey, take Mother home," Brianne suggested as she left. She walked swiftly down the hallway and out the main door. The moment she reached the elevator, she punched the button with more force than was necessary.

"That was quite a show in there," Pete commented. He leaned against the wall with his arms crossed over his chest.

"Diminished capacity, my butt," she muttered, so lost in her own anger she didn't hear his remark.

"What do you intend to do for an encore, princess?" He watched her as if fascinated with this new side to a well-known socialite.

A soft *ping* alerted them to the elevator's arrival just as the doors slid open. Brianne was pleased to see it was empty. She stepped inside with Pete close behind her. As the doors slid closed, she stared at the mirrored interior. Ash blond hair swept in careless array around her shoulders. A body-skimming, hot pink dress showed off her legs and a face that she still wasn't used to seeing in a mirror. For a split second she thought she saw her old self reflected—glossy black hair, arched eyebrows, full mouth always ready to smile and dark eyes filled with rowdy humor. She wasn't sure whether to laugh or cry. She started to stab the button for the garage then halted. She turned her head and stared at Pete, who stared back. For a moment she'd forgotten he was there.

"How about a drink?"

He cocked an eyebrow. "At two-thirty in the afternoon?"

"Sure, why not? It's happy hour on the East Coast." She punched the button for the lobby. "Besides, this way we'll beat the crowd."

Pete allowed Brianne to take the lead as she crossed the lobby toward the large glass doors. When they reached the sidewalk, she looked to her right then her left before heading right. Half a block later, she entered a bar he figured was perfect for yuppies working in the area. Brianne chose a booth near the rear. When the waitress asked them what they'd like, she nodded for Pete to go first.

"I'll have whatever you have on draft," he stated, then looked at Brianne. "What kind of wine do you want?"

"Wine?" She uttered a short laugh before looking up at the waitress. "Not on your life. I'll have a tequila shooter."

Pete felt a roaring in his ears for a moment. He suddenly remembered the night he'd gone out drinking with Allie. She'd been having problems with Whit, and he had gone along to keep her out of trouble. Not that he had to worry about her, he'd soon learned. She dispatched any amorous Romeos with ease and drank him under the table in the process. All evening she'd drunk tequila shooters.

"Funny, I would have pegged you for a wine drinker," he said casually.

She shot him a look filled with disgust. "Not if I can help it."

The waitress set their drinks down. Pete sat back and watched Brianne sprinkle salt on the back of her hand, lick it, down the tequila and then suck a lime wedge with practiced ease.

"Now that is what I call a drink," she murmured.

He felt that roaring in his ears again. Allie had always said that after her first drink. He took a deep breath and reminded himself that he was only thinking that because of guilt. Guilt that he hadn't done anything to save Allie's life. Guilt that he hadn't insisted she not go home that night. Although what he would have done, he wasn't sure. For a long time he'd thought she was one fine-looking woman, but Allie had never seemed to see herself that way. She'd always acted as if she couldn't get anyone better than Whit. Any man she'd been involved with before Whit had been the same—all of them out to use her. He wished he could have shown her she could have had much better than that bastard.

"If they use diminished capacity, you would probably end up with nothing more than a short stay in a fancy hospital, where you could tell the doctor all about your fantasies and you'd be out in six months or so," he said carefully.

She shot him a laserlike look that should have sliced him in two.

"I did not kill him," she stated from between clenched teeth. "And I will not say I was so insane I didn't realize what I was doing when I didn't do it to begin with." Her fingers shook with agitation as they stroked the rim of her glass. She turned her head and gestured to the waitress, indicating that she wished to have a refill. "What is it with people? I thought you were judged innocent until proven guilty."

"I keep telling you it's kind of hard to think a person innocent when they're found with the gun in their hand standing over the body," Pete explained, with logic Brianne didn't want to hear.

She leaned back as another glass was set in front of her, then used the same careless skill to dispatch this drink. Pete sat there watching her, feeling a strong sense of déjà vu. There was something in her eyes. They might be emerald green instead of chocolate brown, but there was still that tug at the back of his mind that brought Allie to his thoughts.

"How did a woman born with a platinum spoon in her mouth end up talking like a tough broad?" he wondered out loud.

"How did a cop end up a P.I.?" she countered.

He started to open his mouth, then snapped it shut. She sure knew how to rattle his cage.

"The hours are better and I don't get shot at as much," he said finally.

"Or perhaps you just didn't like seeing the bad guys get away so much," Brianne murmured. "And this way you don't have to worry about doing everything by the book."

Pete felt that faint, prickling unease again. He'd said something very similar to Allie a year ago right after he resigned. He shoved the thought ruthlessly from his mind.

"Why are we here?" he asked abruptly, picking up his glass and sipping his beer.

Brianne pushed her glass to one side and placed her arms on the table. "I want the name of the baddest, nastiest, most-inhuman criminal attorney you know of. I'm talking about someone you absolutely hate, because they've gotten off people you'd rather have seen put away for good."

Pete couldn't help it. He had to smile at the idea of this social butterfly going up against some of the attorneys he knew.

"You don't want much, do you?"

"Just my life back." For a moment, her smile looked sad. "Except that isn't possible," she murmured to herself, momentarily forgetting he was even there.

He chose not to follow up that remark just yet. "Do you want me to set up the appointment?"

"Would it bother you working for someone you probably don't respect?"

"Not as long as the bills are paid on time." He pulled his wallet out of his pocket and dropped several bills on the table. "Come on, princess. Time to return you to your chariot."

"Why?"

"Because I said so." He grasped her arm and pulled her to her feet.

She fumbled with her purse. "I invited you. I'll pay."

Pete didn't stop as he almost dragged her out of the bar. "Don't worry. I'll put it on my expense account."

"What makes them think they can rule my life?" she asked as they walked back up the street to the parking garage.

"Your mother's obviously paying the bills, and she feels she has the right to have her say."

"Not when I'm the one concerned." Brianne suddenly felt tired and out of sorts. She wanted Mathias to tell her what to do, but there was only silence inside her head.

"What level are you on?" Pete asked. He punched the appropriate button when she told him and leaned against the wall as if nothing was wrong.

Brianne looked at him from under the cover of her lowered lashes. As usual, he was intimidating and gorgeous. Why couldn't she have gone for someone like him instead of Whit? If nothing else, she would still have been alive today.

Except you wouldn't have that incredible wardrobe and a car that starts every time, she mentally reminded herself as she dug through her purse for her keys.

Pete's hand pressed lightly against the small of her back as they walked toward her car. She punched the button to disarm her car alarm and unlock the door.

"I'm sorry this was a wasted trip," she started to tell him, but barely got the words out before his mouth covered hers in a kiss that was dark and probing. Since her mouth was already open, she offered no resistance when his tongue thrust inside to curl around hers. She felt the cool metal of her car at her back and the heat of Pete's body against her front. For once she was willing to dive headlong into the fire. Especially when he was stoking it. His arms curved around her body and pulled her close while his fingers performed a bit of magic, stroking up and down her back, which caused her dress to ride up.

Brianne was dizzy from the numerous sensations rioting through her body. If Brianne Sinclair had ever been repressed before, having Allie in there was making sure that wasn't going to happen anymore! Heat exploded through her body as she hugged Pete against her.

She wanted him! All the time she had known him she had wanted him, but had always refused to admit it. Well, dammit, she was admitting it now!

Except was it Allie who had wanted him so badly or Brianne? For a moment she wasn't sure who she was.

Sanity was slow in taking over. When she finally pulled away from him, she could still taste him on her lips. Could still feel the imprint of his body against hers, especially that hard ridge against the center of her body. She took a shuddering breath, aching to have him within. How could one kiss have so much power over a woman?

She had only to look at him to know he was asking himself the same question. "You going to slap my face?" he asked in a voice husky with desire.

She mutely shook her head.

"Fire me?"

She again shook her head.

He looked wary. It was obvious Pete knew he had acted unprofessionally, but he wasn't about to apologize for his behavior. Little did he know that if he had, she *would* have hit him.

Brianne coughed to clear her throat. "Call the attorney for me and set up an appointment for day after tomorrow," she said in a low voice. "Let me know when and where."

Pete shifted from one foot to the other as if preparing for a fight. "Anything else?"

With a swiftness he hadn't expected, Brianne linked an arm around his neck and pulled his face down for a kiss that quickly turned out to be as hot and sultry as the one he had given her. When she released him, she stepped back and pulled her car door open. Before he had a chance to recover his wits, she had the engine purring and had backed out of the space, driving off with a squeal of tires.

"Damn," he muttered, watching the taillights wink as the car sped down the ramp. "I think I'm in more trouble than she is."

Chapter Seven

Brianne knew something was wrong the moment she stepped inside her sitting room. For a moment she told herself it was nothing more than an abnormal shift in the air. She carefully closed her door and leaned back against it. She barely breathed as she tried to feel a change—anything to indicate why she felt so suspicious. She pushed herself away from the door, walked toward the middle of the room and slowly turned in a tight circle.

Had that porcelain figurine been in that exact spot when she'd left? She already knew the maid hadn't been in to clean. Drawing on a past memory from one of Pete's conversations about how to see if a room had been searched, she took one corner and carefully looked everything over. Hating herself for still feeling paranoid, she gingerly picked up the lamp to see if there was a listening device on the bottom. When she finished going through the room, she moved on to examine her bedroom and bathroom. While some things appeared out of place, nothing rang urgent alarm bells in her mind.

She nearly jumped out of her skin when a soft knock sounded at the door. The maid, whose name she now knew to be Irene, smiled and stepped inside carrying an armload of clothing.

"I'm sorry I couldn't get these put away before you came back upstairs, but I needed to transfer everything onto your hangers," she apologized walking toward the huge walk-in closet. "But I wanted to finish the cleaning first."

Cleaning. She had been cleaning the room! That's why things looked a little out of place! Brianne resisted the urge to laugh hysterically. She kept a smile on her lips as the maid transferred the clothing to the closet.

With an apologetic smile, the woman left the room, carefully closing the door behind her.

"Maid service!" Brianne groaned, dropping backward onto the bed. "How could I forget Brianne wouldn't be cleaning her own room? After all, I thought Brianne Sinclair's life meant parties, trips to Europe, skiing and more parties," she muttered. "So why did she have to do something really stupid like get accused of killing her fiancé just when I'm thrust into her body?" Feeling angry and frustrated, she threw her purse across the room and watched the leather bounce harmlessly against her dresser.

She sat there, legs crossed, top leg swinging to a tune bouncing through her head as she stared at the dresser.

"I wonder if she kept a diary," she murmured to herself. "With her social life, she must have—at least some kind of calendar. She wouldn't want to miss out on anything important. All I have to do is find it. Hey, Mathias. Did she keep a diary?"

Are you asking if you keep a journal?

"When I was sixteen I learned it wasn't a good idea to keep a diary. At least, not where your little brother could find it if he looked hard enough. Kirk Richards never talked to me again after finding out what I thought of him." She jumped up, fully prepared to finish her exploration of the suite. After changing into something more casual, she headed back to the sitting room. The writing desk was her first destination. The top drawer yielded nothing more than pens and pencils, paper clips and notepaper with Brianne's monogram etched in dark blue on the heavy cream stock. She found more stationery in the top side drawer—all monogrammed or sporting her name in elegant calligraphy.

"Obviously, she liked to remind everyone who was writing the note," she muttered, pawing through the various papers until she reached the bottom of the drawer. Nothing.

In a thorough search of all the drawers, Brianne found only financial records stashed in appropriate manila folders, and letters and postcards from friends. Many had *answered* written in one corner with the date.

"Such a neatnik." For lack of a diary to read, she studied the credit-card receipts. "Amazing that with her boring taste in clothes, she could shop so much." She jumped when the telephone chimed. No jarring ring for the Sinclair phones! She already knew Brianne had a private line, and she punched in that button. "Hello?"

"You still willing to see another attorney?"

She had to smile. Pete's voice was music to her ears. "That depends."

"On what?"

"On whether you found me a good one."

"Trust me. He's good," he assured her. "Don't expect him to kowtow to you or hold your hand, because it just isn't in him. He's not Mr. Charm, but he's a damn good attorney. He'll see you tomorrow at ten. Don't forget your checkbook. He doesn't come cheap."

"Have you found out anything else?" she asked.

"I'm seeing a—" he paused and papers rustled in the background "—Lisa Winters this afternoon. I figured I'd see what your friends have to say about you and good ole Michael."

"I hope you've had all your shots," she murmured, gripping a pencil so hard it snapped in half.

"What?"

"Nothing." Brianne sounded unconcerned, while she felt completely the opposite.

"Here's his address. I'll meet you there tomorrow at ten." He reeled off the address of an office building not far from his. "He's real picky about punctuality, so don't be late."

"I am never late," she said huffily.

"And you might want to leave Mom at home this time. Something tells me she and Rhyder wouldn't get along."

"She wasn't invited the last time. I think she's testy because no one has offered her the Mother of the Year award lately. Thank you and goodbye."

Pete chuckled. "Don't worry about Lisa Winters, princess. I learned how to handle women like her years ago. See you in the morning."

It wasn't until she hung up that Brianne realized Pete's comment meant he had heard her.

"Hackett, if you weren't so damned good-looking, I'd fire you." She tossed the paperwork back into her desk without any regard for where it belonged. She only knew she wanted it out of her sight. Determined to find something positive, she went into the bedroom and renewed her search. As she continued looking, she tried to recall where she had heard the name Rhyder before. She knew it wasn't the evening news. Then she remembered times Pete had cursed Rhyder Carson, when the attorney represented some of Pete's arrests. Pete hadn't liked the man, but he had respected him for his thoroughness in each case.

A soft knock at the door startled her. "Miss Sinclair?"

Deep in her walk-in closet, Brianne jumped. "Yes!" She coughed to clear her throat. "Ah, yes?"

"I'm sorry to disturb you, but your mother requested that you come to her sitting room." The woman's voice was apologetic.

"Right now?"

"Yes, ma'am."

Brianne swallowed a sigh. She had already learned that Olivia Sinclair's word was law in the house.

"I'll be right there." She ran her fingers through her hair, ruffling the waves, and stopped in the bathroom long enough to touch up her lipstick. She hoped the added color would make up for her casual clothing, but sincerely doubted it. Not when the color she chose was called Sunburst.

The moment she stepped inside Olivia's sitting room she knew even lipstick wouldn't help the situation. The older woman's eyes frosted over the moment she gazed at her. "I don't believe I've seen that outfit before," she drawled,

Brianne made a quick turn, her arms held out in a model's pose. "I picked it up at the store. Don't you love it?" She smoothed the fuchsia pants that went with a short-sleeved tunic striped with ivory, fuchsia and orange. Her earrings were bold orange-and-fuchsia swirls.

"You look much better in neutral colors."

Brianne recognized an order when she received it. After all, she'd taken more than her share of them over the years. But she was determined not to take any more.

"I was getting tired of wearing nothing but neutrals. After a while they're so bland, don't you think? And shouldn't a member of Sinclairs Department Store always look her best?" She walked over to the delicate settee and sat down. "I understand you wanted to see me?" She decided she would take the direct approach as often as she could. She had an idea it was the only way she could keep her own with Olivia.

Olivia sat in her wheelchair with her back ramrod straight. With the drapes drawn behind her and only one lamp burning in the room, highlighting her black dress, she appeared to be a melodramatic apparition. "I want you to call Joshua first thing tomorrow and apologize to him. You will also explain to him that you will do whatever is necessary to have this incident over and done with. You will defer to his knowledge in these matters.''

Brianne might not have had a temper, but Allie did. And it was Allie's temper that flared. She wanted to knock this high-and-mighty woman off her self-imposed pedestal but good!

"I don't think so, Mother. Personally I don't feel he can handle this case, since he has no criminal-law expertise. Also, I have already retained a new attorney." All right, she didn't know for sure if the man would take her case, but by God, she'd make sure he did!

Olivia sat up even straighter. "Who?"

"Rhyder Carson."

Olivia's nose twitched, as if she smelled something bad. "The man has a reputation for grandstanding. He's only after the money you can pay him and the exposure your case will give him."

"He's representing me. There're no immediate plans for marriage," Brianne quipped, and instantly knew her joke was not well taken.

"Good thing, because it wouldn't be allowed."

She was amused more than irritated by her mother's high-handed manner. Then something in the back of her mind seemed to nudge her.

"Marrying Michael was allowed."

"He came from a good family. He would have had an excellent future with the stores," she declared.

"But there must have been a problem somewhere," Brianne said as casually as possible.

Jessica Fletcher, you're not.

She wished Mathias was visible so she could hit him.

I wouldn't think violent thoughts, Brianne. I'm a necessary evil in your life.

"This isn't a parking ticket, Mother, this is a murder charge," she said bluntly. "Joshua might be able to handle legalities for large corporations, but he has no idea what's involved with criminal law."

"And you think you know?" The woman's sarcasm came with an upper-crust smile.

"I want someone who knows what to look for, and I understand Rhyder Carson is one of the best." Brianne stood up. "Is there anything else?"

Anger was thinly veiled in her eyes. "No." Olivia's hands clutched the wheelchair arms for a moment. She waited until Brianne reached the door before asking. "Who are you?"

Brianne didn't betray any of her thoughts as she turned around. "I am who I've always been. Your daughter. What a shame you refuse to admit that."

Olivia's answering smile was downright deadly. "My Brianne never spoke back to me the way you have. And I can't believe that a simple little knock on the head would change you this drastically." Her gaze wandered over the fuchsia outfit.

"Being accused of murder would drastically change anyone." Brianne twisted the knob and walked out of the room.

She waited until she reached her own bedroom before allowing her knees to collapse. "She knows," she moaned, dropping back on her bed, arms outstretched. "I swear the woman can read minds and she's figured it all out. I'm done for."

Perhaps Brianne needs a little more freedom. A place of her own would take care of that.

"Ha! If I'm not careful, I will have a place of my own. In prison!"

"TELL ME THE TRUTH, Hackett. How did you snag a classy lady like Brianne Sinclair?" Rhyder barked when Pete entered his office.

"I didn't. She came to me." He dropped into the chair opposite Rhyder's desk.

"Can't imagine she was that desperate." Rhyder leaned back in his chair and surveyed a man he now called friend. "Do her pictures in the paper do her justice?"

"You'll see soon enough." Pete glanced down at his watch.

At first glance, Rhyder Carson didn't look the part of a successful criminal attorney. His silver-streaked, raven black hair was long enough to be tied back in an unruly ponytail. Instead of a three-piece suit worthy of Savile Row, he wore a pair of faded jeans and a black cotton shirt with the sleeves rolled to the elbow. No manicure for this man. He had calluses on his palms and fingertips better suited to someone who worked on a shipping dock than in an office.

Privately, Pete saw Rhyder as a wild animal that needed to be out in the open instead of confined in a courtroom. He'd once tried to indulge his curiosity about Rhyder by tapping into various databases. All he'd learned was that he was a man to be reckoned with. Especially since, two hours after he performed his computer games, Rhyder came to call on him and softly suggested he not try that again. Pete didn't. He had enough answers. For now.

When Pete left the force and later got his private investigator's license, Rhyder was one of the first to contact him, asking if he'd take on a case for him. Pete worked for the man off and on after that. Slowly, their working relationship bonded into a close friendship.

"What have you learned about her so far?" Rhyder asked, leaning back in his chair with one ankle braced on the opposite knee.

"I've learned that the people she associates with couldn't be considered friends of any kind." Pete made a face. "I talked to a woman yesterday who was more interested in getting me into bed than answering my questions. Although she did say something about telling me anything I'd want to know. As long as I asked them in her bedroom."

Rhyder chuckled. "How was she?"

"Are you kidding? She might have been gorgeous, but I'm not that desperate." He shuddered dramatically. "Talk about scary."

Rhyder smiled. "Sounds like my kind of woman."

"Naw, even you would draw the line with that one. I tell you, Brianne Sinclair doesn't have friends. She has acquaintances who would make great enemies." Pete shook his head. "The evidence is damning, but I still feel she didn't do it."

Rhyder nodded, familiar with his friend's hunches. Hunches that were ninety-nine percent on the mark. "What else do you feel about her?"

Pete wasn't about to tell him he'd kissed her. And wouldn't have minded doing even more. "There's something about her." He shook his head, as if unsure where to begin. "She doesn't drink fancy wines. She drinks tequila shooters. Her speech is more down to earth and direct than you'd expect for someone who got most of her education in Europe. I listen to what people say about her and it doesn't jive with the woman I've seen and talked to. It's as if she's two different people."

Rhyder's lips twisted. "Maybe she is. It wouldn't be anything new."

He shook his head. "I don't know. Maybe you'll see something I haven't."

A soft knock at the door alerted them they wouldn't be alone for much longer.

"Miss Sinclair is here," Sofia, Rhyder's secretary, informed them after opening the door and looking in. Even she, with her swinging multibraids, skintight red T-shirt, black spandex ankle-length pants and red spike heels didn't look as if she belonged there.

"Send her in," Rhyder directed.

Both men watched the door as it opened wider, and Brianne walked in.

Pete knew most women would have been intimidated by entering a room he and Rhyder occupied. He'd seen it many times when he and Rhyder spent the evening nursing beers down at The Mug House. One of their favorite watering holes, it offered several pool tables in the back, great drinks, a bartender who didn't bother you and a jukebox that didn't play any tunes recorded before 1972. No disco there. He didn't have to worry about Brianne. It was obvious she could handle herself just fine.

"Since I'm already familiar with Pete, you must be Mr. Carson." She stepped forward and offered her hand.

"Which makes you Ms. Sinclair." Rhyder folded his hand around hers.

"I answer to Bri much easier." She took the chair Rhyder gestured toward.

"Would you care for some coffee?"

"That would be nice, thank you." She gave him a thousand-watt smile, which dimmed a bit when she turned to Pete. "How was your meeting with Lisa?"

Pete shrugged. "Interesting."

She straightened up. "Meaning?"

"Meaning she can say a lot of words about being one of your closest friends while really saying she hates your guts and hopes you get the gas chamber since she had the hots for your fiancé."

She didn't look a bit surprised. "I always thought I felt as if I had a knife in my back when I was around her."

Rhyder waited until Sofia set coffee cups in front of all three of them. He pulled out a yellow legal pad and a pen.

"I have to admit your case interests me," he told Brianne. "You were found next to the body with the murder weapon in your hand, yet, from the beginning, you've insisted you're innocent. You're either very clever or very stupid."

"And you haven't decided which one yet, right?" She picked up her cup and sipped the dark brew. "That's fine. I'm still trying to figure it all out myself."

Pete just sat back and watched. It wasn't difficult to do, since Brianne was wearing a cobalt blue dress that showed off her legs as she crossed them. He watched the top leg swing to a beat she apparently heard inside her head as she talked to Rhyder. The longer he studied her, the more something nagged at the back of his mind. Something familiar about her that he couldn't quite pin down. He shifted in his chair.

Oh hell! Maybe it was the fact he wanted to see what was under those clothes. To find out why she'd changed from a plain moth into a butterfly so quickly. Although plain was never a word he would have used to describe her. He silently cursed the tight fit of his jeans as he sat there. Then cursed Rhyder, when he saw the knowing look the man shot him. Some kind of professional he was if he couldn't keep his hormones under wraps for more than a couple of seconds.

For the next two hours, Rhyder questioned Brianne carefully, occasionally pausing to make notes on the pad in front of him.

"Why do you think someone would want to kill your fiancé and pin it on you?" he finally asked.

Brianne thought about it and slowly shook her head. "I have no idea," she admitted.

He looked at her long and hard. "Why do I have trouble believing you?"

"Because I can't give you the answers you want, so you figure I'm either lying or just acting stupid," she said without hesitation. The entire time her gaze was steady, no change in facial expression or body language. She was telling him all she knew. "When the doctor examined me, he said I was suffering from shock. All I know is that the events of that night are wiped out as if someone had used an eraser on my brain. All I remember is my brother and sister-in-law asking me what happened. Trey said when he came upon me, I just looked at him and fainted.''

Rhyder made a few more notes. "I'll be honest with you. No attorney in his right mind would want this case. There's too much evidence against you. And there's the word out how you two hadn't been getting along for several weeks before your fiancé's death. The rumors your engagement was going to be broken. Not to mention you do know how to use a gun.''

"Are you in your right mind, Mr. Carson?" Brianne asked quietly.

A smile softened his harsh features. "I always thought I was, but I'm beginning to doubt it. Because I will take your case. I only ask one thing of you. You are to be honest with me all the way. We've got a lot of work ahead of us." He glanced at Pete.

"She's already hired me," Pete said amiably.

"Then I guess we have a deal. I'll have my secretary draw up a contract." Rhyder reached across his desk with his hand outstretched.

Brianne's hand was engulfed by his. "I just bet you're hell on wheels in the courtroom," she said with a smile.

Rhyder smiled back. "And I bet you're hell on wheels at society balls."

"No, when I'm there, I tend to hide my light under a bushel basket." Brianne stood up. She barely glanced at Pete. "No use in making them think I'm one of them."

"Why don't you wait outside for me for a minute?" Pete asked abruptly, breaking into the conversation without regard to etiquette.

Brianne turned on her heel and stared at him from under an arched eyebrow. "Certainly, sir," she murmured. She turned back to the lawyer. "Thank you for your assistance, Rhyder."

"Any time, Brianne."

Pete waited until the door closed behind her. "Man, you two got chummy real fast," he grumbled.

"Jealous?" Rhyder threw down the verbal glove.

Pete used a gesture not appreciated by most of the population, but Rhyder merely laughed.

"Does anyone know about your double life?" Pete challenged. "No self-respecting dad should be lusting after a client."

"Neither should a self-respecting private eye," he countered.

Pete stood up and leaned forward, planting his hands flat on the desktop. His expression was steely, the kind that had had more than one criminal cowering in his boots.

Rhyder didn't even blink. "She's got guts, Pete," he said quietly. "It's a good thing she does, because the police are convinced she's guilty."

"But you're like me. You don't think she did it."

"If there's positive proof she's guilty, I'll turn in my law degree," he stated. "You're right. She's very direct. And I can't believe she'd kill the man when all she'd have to do is give him back his ring and kick him out of the house." He glanced at his calendar. "Can you be here tomorrow afternoon around three with whatever you've picked up so far?"

Pete didn't have to look at a calendar to know he had the time free. "No problem." He ambled toward the door.

"Hey, Pete."

Pete looked over his shoulder.

"Try and keep the libido under control until we have a not-guilty verdict," Rhyder advised.

"Are you going to be able to?" he countered.

"I'm not the one who's hot for the lady."

Pete chuckled. "Maybe we were star-crossed lovers in another life or something. Although the lady is way out of my league."

"I think she'd disagree with you on that score."

"Yeah, well, that would be one time she'd lose," he muttered, walking out.

The first thing Pete saw when he stepped out of the office was Brianne standing by Sofia's desk, talking animatedly to the younger woman. Most women in her social sphere wouldn't have given the secretary the time of day.

"Come on, I'll walk you to your car," he said, gesturing toward the door.

Brianne studied him as they walked out to the elevator and descended four floors. The building had been built in a grander, more-elegant age, with an elevator that resembled an ornate cage instead of a steel box.

"You don't seem very happy that Rhyder's taking my case," she said, breaking the silence.

"No, I'm glad he's representing you. He'll do a good job."

"Then what's wrong?"

He always hated women who could sense when something was wrong. Why couldn't they just ignore him when he felt like this? He jammed his hands in his jacket pockets as they walked out of the building and around the corner to the parking lot.

"Rhyder does a good job because he has three kids counting on him."

Brianne didn't blink at his abrupt statement. "Is there something wrong with that?"

"Just thought you should know."

"Meaning don't flirt with the man because his wife might come after me?"

"No wife. Just kids."

Brianne stopped at her car and disengaged the alarm. "Don't worry, I'm through with tall-dark-and-dangerous types."

Before she could open her door, he had her trapped between the door and his body, his arms bracketing her sides.

"Funny. I never thought that guy was all that dangerous," he murmured, leaning in more than close enough to smell her perfume. He didn't think there was anything that smelled better. He lowered his head as if to kiss her.

"No, but you are." With a smile, she dipped down and around her door. "Oh, and Pete, I want to come along on any more interviews you do on my behalf. I'd hate to think any of my friends would get the wrong idea."

He straightened up. "About me?"

Laughter danced in her eyes. "Only that you're easy prey. And not all of them have had their shots." She swiftly leaned forward and pressed a light kiss against his mouth. "Call me."

He stood there watching her drive off. He had to admire the way she jetted out into the heavy traffic.

"Calling you is the least of my problems."

Chapter Eight

"What the hell are you trying to do?"

Brianne turned around to discover Trey barreling down the hallway, obviously looking for her. She remained rooted to the spot, except she wasn't about to allow him to browbeat her the way their mother did. She crossed her arms in front of her chest, not as a defensive measure but as an impatient one. Hell, she had things to do, and letting Trey yell at her wasn't one of them!

"What now?" she demanded without waiting to hear from him first. There was no way she was going to let him intimidate her. If Olivia couldn't do it, what made Trey think he could?

He practically slid to a halt, taken aback by her blunt manner. Confusion marred his good looks, as if he was gazing at someone he didn't know.

Brianne hid her smile. Little did he realize that he really *didn't* know her! Still clothed in his charcoal, pinstriped suit, white shirt and tasteful blue-and-dark-gray-striped tie, he looked as fresh and crisp as he had that morning. Not for the first time, she wondered why he and his wife lived with his mother when they could easily afford a place of their own.

Ah, yes, the dutiful son. Don't you realize that if Trey is living here, he can keep a closer eye on his mother's medication?

Trey leaned forward, deliberately invading her space. "Do you realize how much you upset Mother by walking out on Joshua yesterday?" he rasped. "Not to mention your hiring that sorry excuse for a private investigator. How could you do that?"

She looked him square in the eye. And delighted in seeing that he had trouble meeting her gaze.

"You know, Trey, you're really ticking me off," she said in a low, even voice. Her smile belied her words. "I hired Mr. Hackett because he has an excellent background in homicide investigations. After all, that was his job when he worked for the police department. Do you realize the man has commendations up the whazoo? He held one of the highest arrest-and-conviction rates even if some of his methods were considered unconventional. He has also found an attorney who is experienced in criminal law, not someone who merely thinks he is. I refuse to stand up in court and say I was suffering from PMS or ate too much sugar or was just plain deranged, so please forgive me for shooting my fiancé. Because I didn't shoot him." This time she was the one to lean forward, invading his space. "Since you and Sheila were here, you must have an idea who really did it."

Trey's eyes turned frosty. "This is not a joking matter, Brianne," he said coldly. "You know very well Sheila and I were attending the fund-raiser for Senator Thompson. When we arrived home, we heard shots and ran into the study, where we found you with Michael. You had a strange look on your face, stared at us and then fainted." He retreated two steps. "Why you have to discuss this now, I don't know. But I suggest you start thinking about your defense, because that sleazy detective and his equally slimy attorney friend aren't going to be able to get you out of this. And if you turn this into a media circus, you'd better not expect Mother to make things right." He smirked, as if expecting his threat to mean something to her.

Brianne assumed it might have meant something to the old Brianne, but she was made of tougher stuff. After being killed by her boyfriend, nothing could bother her!

"I don't expect her to do anything but offer moral support. Now if you don't mind, I'd like to change for dinner." She flashed him a brief smile and turned around, heading for her bedroom.

"This isn't like you, Brianne," Trey called after her.

She looked over her shoulder as she reached her bedroom door. "What is like me?"

He shook his head. "Not what I'm seeing now."

"Good, because there just happens to be a new Brianne Sinclair in town." She twisted the knob and opened the door, wiggling her fingers in a saucy wave as she disappeared into her room.

She didn't think it was over. And from the moment she sat down to dinner, she knew she was right. Olivia conducted the meal in cold silence, echoed by Trey's equally frosty demeanor. Sheila's wary glances bounced from one to the other as she nibbled on her salad and ate only a few bites of the main course, in deference to her eternal battle to keep her size-six figure. "I must say the brighter colors do more for your complexion," she said brightly, nibbling a cucumber round as she studied Brianne's watermelon silk dress with its cobalt blue belt adding that extra zing. Her earrings and bracelet were the same bold blue color.

"She would be better off in conservative colors," Olivia stated in her I-have-spoken voice.

"I don't know, I think the world looks brighter this way," Brianne said cheerfully. But as the evening wore on, she felt as if her bold facade was going to crumble.

"I understand the police are interviewing all our friends and business associates," Olivia commented, staring at Brianne.

"They plan to conduct a thorough investigation." Trey chimed in, also looking at his sister. "Bri, they're not going to accept your amnesia story much longer. Not with what was going on between you and Michael."

Her head swiveled around. "Meaning?"

He shifted uncomfortably under her gaze, as he often did with his mother. "You know what I mean," he mumbled, turning back to his roast lamb.

"No, Trey, I don't," Brianne said slowly and distinctly. "Why don't you enlighten me?"

"There will be no more talk about this disgusting incident," Olivia commanded. "It was bad enough that you rejected Joshua's expert advice. I don't care to hear how you'll be handling this from now on."

"Did you hear our Junior League is sponsoring this year's symphony ball?" Sheila interjected, casting megawatt smiles around. "We're meeting tomorrow to plan the theme. Renee Mainwaring suggested Springtime in Paris. Wouldn't that be lovely?''

''Don't tell me. Are you going to import the Eiffel Tower or just have it sculpted in ice?''

Sheila stared at Brianne with a hurt expression on her face. ''You've always adored helping us plan our functions.''

She marveled that her sister-in-law could look crushed without moving one facial muscle. She wondered if Sheila had opted for plastic surgery yet. She couldn't believe a woman's face could be that perfect. ''If you'll excuse me, I have some calls to make,'' she said as she got to her feet.

Olivia didn't look up. ''We haven't had dessert yet.''

Brianne's gaze swiveled from one to the other. ''I've had enough.''

''I do not appreciate your attitude,'' Olivia announced as her daughter walked out of the dining room.

''Then try to remember I'm of legal age.''

Brianne ascended the stairs and hurried to her suite. Once there, she pulled a bottle of wine out of the small refrigerator and poured herself a glass. She flipped through the television channels, but found nothing that could hold her interest.

She curled up in the large easy chair with its matching square ottoman, starring blindly at a sitcom that didn't bring one laugh to her lips.

''Usually, I could call Lil and we'd go to a movie or shopping,'' she said out loud, as she sipped her wine. ''Or I'd talk Whit into going to a club and we'd dance until closing time.'' A lump settled in the pit of her stomach. ''And there was that time Abby, Gail, Lil and I went to that hockey game.'' She sniffed. ''We had a lot of fun that night. We always had fun when we had a girls' night out. And now I can't even call them. It isn't fair that I can remember them and all they remember about me is my funeral.'' She curled her lip. ''Pete better find out Whit killed me or I'm going to be very upset. I mean, I'm prime evidence for that murder and there's no way I could get anyone to believe me!''

What do you think you're doing?

''I'm feeling sorry for myself. And I don't want to hear any lectures about it, either. I deserve this episode of self-pity.'' She wiped the back of her hand across her nose. ''I'm sitting here watching TV when I'd rather be out doing something.''

Then do just that.

''I can't when I don't have any friends to call and go out with.''

You have a lot of friends. Brianne Sinclair is a very popular woman.

''Says you.'' She took another sip of wine. ''The only calls I've gotten are from people who want all the gory details. At least Lisa stopped by. But she only wanted gory details, too. She was just more up-front about it.''

I'd say she was curious to see if you were pale and pining away. I'm sure she was very disappointed to see you looking so well.

''I just wish she could have dropped some hints to help me out with this disaster.'' Brianne's shoulders lifted and fell as she sighed. ''Mathias, I have to know what happened between Brianne and Michael that night.''

That is something you need to learn on your own.
"Why?"
It's the rules.
"They're not my rules!" She rolled her wineglass between her palms. "This isn't fair to me and it isn't fair to Pete. He needs me to answer questions that I can't answer."
You've done a good job so far.
"But it can't last. I know he thinks I'm deliberately evading some of his questions. He probably thinks I'm guilty!"
If he thought you were guilty he wouldn't have taken the case.
Brianne's lips twisted in a humorless smile. "Yes, he would, because the money I'm paying him is giving him enough income so he can take time to find proof that Whit killed me."
That's your real problem, isn't it? Pete.
She felt dejected enough to cry. "I always liked him. He's the best guy I ever knew."
Then why didn't you do something about it when you had the chance?
She settled for another sip of wine, which was better than crying. "I didn't do anything because I wasn't good enough for him. He was a cop, a detective, and I was a waitress in a coffee shop no sane person would work in. Not a lot of education except for what I learned by reading the newspaper and news magazines during my coffee and meal breaks."
Then why did you work there? Why not do something about your prospects?
Brianne wrinkled her nose. "I wasn't about to leave when I had the chance to see Pete just about every

day," she admitted in a low voice. "He was there for at least one meal a day because he lived near there."

He asked you to have dinner with him one time and you turned him down in such a way he never asked you out again. I'm surprised the two of you remained friends.

She tipped her head back and stared up at the ceiling, which was better than looking at the characters on TV. She had no idea where the voice came from other than inside her head. "How did you know that?"

I know everything.

"Smart aleck," she muttered. "All right, yes, he asked me out and I turned him down. The guy had just gotten a commendation a few weeks before. He was written up in the paper. He only asked me out because he'd recently broken up with Karen. He wanted to make sure he was still attractive to women. I don't know why, when he could have any woman he wanted. He didn't really want me. Anyone would have done that night."

That's what you think.

The knot in her stomach was rapidly growing and turning to acid. "I always blow it with men. There was Jerry. Remember him?" She waved her wine glass around for emphasis. "The man was pure slime! He'd go on about all the travel he had to do, but wanted to see me every Wednesday and Thursday. How did I know he had a wife and three kids tucked away in the Valley?"

What about Ted?

"Ugh! What a mistake he was!" She made a face. "Do you know he actually tried on my underwear?" She took another sip for emphasis. Noting the low level in her glass, she refilled it. "He even put on that red bustier I'd gotten at Victoria's Secret! And that was brand-new! I couldn't wear it after that." This time she took a hefty swallow. She blinked several times. "Does Brianne wear glasses?"

She has twenty-twenty vision. Perhaps your fuzzy vision has something to do with what you're drinking.

"I rarely drink, and when I do, I never get drunk." She held her glass up in front of her face. "Of course, I never drink wine."

And Brianne never drank tequila shooters. You shouldn't have done it that day when you were with Pete.

"Never had a tolerance for wine." To prove her point, she took another swallow. "Maybe more of Allie jumped in here than just her brain."

You aren't doing yourself any good, you know.

"Then give me something to work on!"

Ask me a logical question, and perhaps I will.

She thought for a moment. "Was Brianne going to break off her engagement to Michael?"

She wasn't happy.

"That's no answer." Brianne set the glass down on the table and got up. She grabbed hold of the chair arm for balance as the room briefly spun around her. "Whoa! That is some wine."

She made her way into the bedroom and stripped off her clothing. Deciding a fuzzy head wasn't a good idea, she took a quick cold shower and slipped on a nightgown and robe.

This time, she chose a diet cola as she settled in front of the TV. She flipped channels until she found "NYPD Blue."

"Much better," she proclaimed, sinking back in the chair. "Now this is quality programming."

PETE HAD LEARNED a long time ago that his best sources of information only came out at night. This time, he chose a rock club he knew Whit hung out at a lot. Whit used to come here sometimes with Allie, many times without, Pete had discovered. That was something he had never told Allie and now wished he had. Maybe if she'd known Whit regularly two-timed her, she would have thrown him out on his sorry butt long ago.

He walked up to the bar and ordered draft beer. The bartender, sporting a cobra tattoo curled around a beefy biceps, drew the beer and placed the mug in front of him.

"Well, hi there." A woman with short blond hair punctuated with dark roots sidled up to him. Her sheer black blouse proved she wasn't wearing a bra, and only two strategic patch pockets kept her from being arrested. Her white leather micromini displayed a pair of long legs encased in black stockings. She batted heavily mascaraed lashes at him. "I can't believe someone like you is here alone."

Pete treated her to a smile to take the sting out of his rejection. "Sorry, sweetheart, the wallet's tapped out."

She smiled back, not insulted by his implication. "Honey, for you it would be free."

"He's a cop, Lucy," the bartender told her.

She sighed heavily with disappointment. "The good ones usually are." She turned away.

"I'm not one anymore," Pete told the man.

"Yeah, but she's like a Gila monster when she sees a good-looking guy," he answered. "Once she latches on, nothing gets her away from you. Besides, I figure you're here for more than a beer, since I've never seen you around before."

Pete hoped the man would prove to be on the up-and-up. "Whit Richards."

He muttered several choice curses under his breath. "The guy's poison."

"Tell me something I don't know. Such as Allie Walker."

"Sam, I need two seven-and-sevens, vodka on the rocks and scotch, no ice," a waitress called out, coming to stand next to Pete. She shot him a quick smile to show she was interested, but didn't appear affronted when he didn't respond in kind.

The bartender held up a finger to say hold on a moment. He quickly mixed the drinks and placed them on a tray for the waitress. Then he leaned across the bar so as not to be overheard by any of the patrons sitting nearby.

"Whit killed Allie," he said in a low voice.

Pete dared not hope it could be this easy. "How do you know? He say so?"

"Hell no, but I know he did. He was fooling around with some chick who came around here a lot." The bartender shook his head, disgust written on his face. "She was some hot number, but she was also trouble. She liked nothing more than to get a couple guys panting after her and start a fight. She hung around

Whit 'cause he threw around enough money to make it worthwhile.''

Pete glanced around. "She in here tonight?"

Sam shook his head. "I heard she's over in the county lockup. She has a habit of putting the wrong thing up her nose. Her name's Gloria Adams."

"Anything else you can tell me?" Pete asked, grateful the man was so open and naturally wondering why.

"Hey man, we all liked Allie," he said gruffly, shaking his head. "She was good people. You want witnesses to say they saw Whit kill her, you've got 'em."

"If only it was that easy," Pete muttered.

"I tried to get her to go out with me a few times," Sam admitted. "You know, it was weird. Sometimes she acted as if she thought she wasn't good enough for me. For a woman who had such street smarts about everyone else, she sure missed out when it came to herself." He looked around the room. "A couple times, I think I'll see her coming through that door. Hard to believe I won't." He shook his head again.

Pete pulled out his wallet and extracted a few bills, holding them out. Sam recoiled.

"Hey, man, don't insult me! I want to see that bastard nailed to the wall."

Pete nodded and settled for digging out one of his business cards. "If you hear anything else, will you let me know?" he requested.

Sam slipped the card into his shirt pocket. "No problem."

Pete finished his beer and walked out of the bar. He studied the list he'd made up, thanks to Lil and a few others. He figured he could handle three more places before the night was over.

When a red car roared down the street, the thought of Brianne Sinclair came to mind. Working days on her case and nights on Allie's was starting to take its toll.

He stared up at the sky. With the streetlights throwing out their orange glow, he couldn't see any stars.

"Allie, I could use some help down here. Even one little sign wouldn't hurt," he said out loud. "Just a hint. In fact, if you could throw a few clues for Brianne Sinclair, I wouldn't mind that, either. Something tells me the two of you would like each other. Still, I wouldn't worry, lady. Her life has turned out not to be all you would have wanted it to be. Believe me, you're better off not being her, after all." He walked over to his Porsche and climbed in. As he drove off, he started hoping he'd run into Whit at one of the clubs. Putting a dent in the bastard's face would make him feel a hell of a lot better right now.

When Pete finally got back to his apartment, it was almost three a.m. and he felt dead on his feet. The counter on his answering machine told him he had four calls. He thought about waiting to hear them after he'd had some sleep, then decided he'd rather get it over with now. He punched the replay button and headed for the kitchen.

Beep!

"Pete, it's Rhyder. I talked to Rick. This guy is convinced they've got an airtight case. Call me so we can go over a few things."

Beep!

"Peter, you know very well I hate talking to these machines." A woman's voice filled the room. He immediately cringed and set his can of beer back in the refrigerator. "Would it hurt you to call your mother more than a few times a year? Just to assure her you're still alive and well? And I do mean in good health, without one broken bone in your body. I only hope that you hear this message, instead of some policeman eavesdropping because you're lying in the hospital. I would love to hear from you before Mother's Day."

He swore under his breath. No one could make him feel guilty the way his mother did.

Beep!

"Pete, Rhyder again. You're not staking out an erring spouse, are you? Call me first thing in the morning," the man's clipped voice ordered.

"Man, when you get a new case you get real testy," Pete muttered, pulling the can of beer out of the fridge again.

Beep!

"Pete, it's Brianne Sinclair." He would have known that voice anywhere. He hated it that she made him think of silk sheets on a hot summer night. "I realize you might not have come up with anything new just yet, but I'd like to talk to you about this. I still want to help you with the investigation. Unless, of course, my mother scared you off. She's been known to do that."

"Yeah, I bet she was a hit when she used to host the midnight monster movie," Pete muttered. "And no, you're not helping. You're the client and you're supposed to let me do the work."

"I'd appreciate a call when you get a chance. I'll be at the store tomorrow all day," she informed him. "Good night."

He waited, hearing the soft click of the machine cutting off the call. "Damn, she's not going to make it easy for any of us. Especially me."

Chapter Nine

"What the hell makes you think you can investigate a crime?" Pete's deep voice rumbled in Brianne's ear.

Awakened out of a sound sleep by the phone, she fumbled with the receiver and put it back to her ear.

"Huh?"

"That's what I'm talking about, Princess. You can't even speak coherently, yet you expect to play private investigator."

"Just a minute," Brianne mumbled. She set the receiver on the bed, pushed her hair away from her face, took several deep breaths and widened her eyes to dramatic widths. She picked up the phone again and cradled it against her shoulder, then said, "Hello, Brianne isn't able to take your call right now. At the tone please leave your name, telephone number and a brief message. Now, take the phone away from your ear." Then she put her fingers between her lips and emitted a shrill whistle. She smiled as she heard his pithy curses.

"Dammit!" Pete shouted. "What're you trying to do? Break my eardrums?"

"I warned you to take the receiver away from your ear," she replied. "That's a reminder. Don't call me at six o'clock in the morning again or you'll get worse."

"Damn, my ears are ringing," he grumbled. "When I get a call at six a.m. in regards to you, you better believe I'll be calling you right afterward."

She sat up at that piece of news. "Someone called you about me? Who?"

"Beats me. They didn't leave a name, and they disguised their voice enough that I couldn't tell if it was a man or woman."

Brianne gripped the receiver until her knuckles turned white. "What did the person say?" she demanded.

"Asked me to find out why you and lover boy were having problems. That once I learn the truth I'll know who killed him."

Brianne exhaled a deep sigh. "Nothing about my innocence?"

"No, sweetheart, nothing about your innocence," he said patiently. "Why, was something supposed to be said about your innocence? What's going to happen? I'm suddenly going to get a notarized statement by special messenger pointing out why you're innocent?"

"You are a very obnoxious man first thing in the morning," she said slowly and distinctly. "Tell you what. You go have three or four cups of coffee to help you turn into a human being again, while I have my own coffee and wake up as my lovely, sweet self. Call me at the store later this morning." She hung up with an audible click.

Brianne sat up in bed, having no idea that Pete was staring at the receiver as if it didn't belong to him.

"Hell, if that didn't sound like Allie," he muttered. "I really need to catch up on my sleep."

BRIANNE SENSED A DIFFERENCE the moment she walked into the store. And she didn't think it was entirely due to her short-sleeved, sun yellow dress with an attached, soutache-trimmed vest that swept over her slim figure and stopped a few inches above her knees.

Honestly, Brianne, you should have livened up your wardrobe years ago, she thought to herself.

May I remind you yet again that you are *Brianne. You really must stop thinking of yourself in the third person.*

She smiled and nodded toward clerks and department managers as she made her way through the store.

It's not easy to remember who I am when I see myself one way and the world sees me another way.

Why are you so worried when you have the ability to change things?

"That's true," she said out loud. She almost laughed at the expression on the jewelry-counter manager's face as she passed by him. "It's true that diamonds are a woman's best friend," she explained, gesturing toward the ad in the morning paper detailing the store's diamond sale. The man had spread it out on top of the glass counter.

It's nice to see that you think so quickly on your feet.

With you, it's a good thing I do, she mentally transmitted to Mathias.

She kept her smile firmly pasted on her lips as she walked toward the bank of elevators. She was grateful to find the one she got into remained empty as it shot upward. Keeping her Brianne face on was proving to be very tiring at times.

"Good morning, Gwen," she said to her secretary.

"Ms. Sinclair." The woman's wide-eyed gaze held a note of caution.

Brianne stopped in front of her desk and tapped her fingers against the top. "What's wrong?"

Gwen leaned across and whispered, "There's a man waiting for you inside your office. I told him it wasn't proper for him to wait in there, but he said it was all right with you. Should I have called Security?"

Her finger tapping increased in tempo. "Tall, sandy brown hair, gray eyes, killer smile?"

The secretary's head bobbed up and down.

Brianne glanced upward for a moment, as if she was having a silent conversation with someone. "Don't worry about it. He doesn't believe in taking no for an answer. I'll handle this."

She swept on past the desk and pushed open her office door. She showed no surprise at finding Pete comfortably ensconced in her chair, his booted feet propped on the desktop.

"This is incredible reading. Better than the mystery I've been into lately. Especially since I guessed the killer's identity on the first page." He held up a sheaf of papers. "I figured stores marked up their products, but not this much. How in the hell do you stay in business?"

"Do you mind?" She snatched the papers out of his hand and set them in her In basket. "Those are private."

He shrugged, unconcerned by her anger. "How can I find out about you if I don't go through your files?" He allowed his gaze to move from the top of her head to the toes of her bright yellow pumps. "Hmm, maybe I should start calling you Mary Sunshine."

She felt the warmth of his gaze all the way through the marrow of her bones and basked in it. "Why are you here?"

Pete didn't bother taking his feet off her desk, so she pushed them off and tipped the chair forward so far he either had to get out or fall out.

"You said to call you at the store. Since I was out and about, I figured I'd stop by instead." He held up his watch. "Do you realize what time it is? Man, you store executives keep great hours. I should have gone into merchandising."

Brianne crossed her arms in front of her, one hip cocked as she tapped her toe against the carpet. Her entire manner indicated he'd better get to the point before she threw something at him.

"I figured I'd do some nosing around the store and see what people have to say about you and Michael," he told her.

"Michael didn't work out of this store."

"No, but you do, and I wanted to see what gossip about the two of you was floating around here. I've already been out to the two stores he was in charge of to hear what they have to say about him."

She wanted to scream. Couldn't he come right out and reveal something without giving all these hints? "And?"

"And," he drawled, "the man was a saint. A prince. The best boss to work for. Courteous. A regular guy. Never asked his girls to stay late unless it was for a very good reason. You name it. Of course, that's what the women said about him." He paused, smiling at Brianne with a male innocence that was totally false.

Her expression let him know she didn't buy his angelic countenance. That she knew no male could claim innocence from the day he was born.

"But the men didn't say the same thing about him, right?" She spun the chair around and settled in the soft leather seat. She leaned back, crossing her legs, then smiled as she noticed his gaze anchor on where her dress rode up a few inches. Allie had always been proud of her legs and was grateful Brianne's were just as good.

Pete perched his hip on the edge of the desk. He picked up the letter opener, tested the tip against his fingers and tried to balance it on one. When that failed, he flipped it end over end. With a hint of a ladylike snarl, Brianne snatched the letter opener from his hands and pointed the sharp end at his chest. He grinned and shrugged, holding his hands up in surrender.

"That's right. He was not a popular guy with his own sex," he stated, now all-business. He leaned forward, resting his arm on the thigh braced on the desk. "Starting off with the news that he wasn't the one who really ran that store. His assistant did. Michael was great at schmoozing with vendors, hitting on the female ones, and preening in front of any mirror he passed. He was convinced your brother would hand over the reins to the empire, when you were married, because Michael considered himself the brains and beauty of Sinclairs, while your brother did nothing more than slog along in the last century the way your father had. Not to mention that Trey would really like nothing more than to take off to the Caribbean with his secretary, except he's scared to death of your mother. For a lady in a wheelchair living on some pretty heavy-duty medication, she's a formidable witch. And that was the politest description of the woman I heard.''

Brianne waited. She knew there was more. Something deep inside nudged her into asking, ''What else did you hear?''

She could have sworn the glimmer in Pete's eyes resembled pity. She hated him for it. ''What?'' she persisted.

''As far as anyone is concerned, you're nothing more than a name in this organization. You have a title but no power. You have no real duties to perform and people tend to ignore you. Your secretary is out there for show. You may sign things, but that's only because your brother wants you to feel useful,'' he said bluntly. ''You do better organizing charity events with your sister-in-law, who, in everyone's opinion, is a typical social butterfly, happy with her life-style. You show up here when it suits you and don't when you feel you have something better to do. Your hobby is shopping, and it appears no one can shop the way you do. Your most-recent spree was the talk of the town.

Did you really spend that much money?'' He shook
his head in mock amazement.

Her face could have been carved from stone. Not by
a blink of the eye had she given any indication of how
his words affected her. Except it wasn't just anyone
looking at Brianne just then, it was Pete. And what he
saw tore at him. What he had just said bothered her,
he could tell. It bothered her a lot.

He didn't stop to think about his actions. With his
usual fluid grace, he was on his feet and had her out
of her chair and in his arms before she could react.
''Hey, what do they know?'' he soothed in a low
voice, rubbing her back with slow, steady sweeps of his
hand.

''They know more than you think.'' She sniffed
once or twice, then rested her cheek against the curve
of his shoulder and slid her arms around his waist. The
man felt so damn good!

''Such as?''

''I can't be useless,'' she continued, in her misery
not hearing his question. ''It's not right. I wasn't supposed to be such a loser. I should be this wonderful
person that others like and admire. I don't want to be
pitied.''

Pete's comforting hand slowed as he listened to her
words. ''You're confusing me here. What do you
mean, you weren't supposed to be a loser? Not that
anyone said you were,'' he hastily added.

''Yes, they did.'' She disengaged herself from his
arms. Her misery was now apparent. ''They're saying
Brianne Sinclair can't do anything more than shop and
look pretty for newspaper photographers. No wonder
Trey is having trouble. He doesn't have anyone to

count on. It's already apparent he didn't even have Michael on his side. Well, things are going to change around here." She dipped her head and a steely look entered her eyes. "For once I'm going to show the world that a talent for shopping can have its uses." She looked down at her desk, sadly cleared of paper. She picked up her phone and punched out Trey's private line. "Hi, it's me. Yes, your sister." She rolled her eyes. "What are you doing for lunch?" She waited a beat. "Sounds boring to me. I have a better idea. No, I'm not going to tell you right now, but come by my office at twelve-thirty. I'll tell you then. And be prepared to be gone for a few hours. Trust me, you won't regret it." After disconnecting, she punched out her secretary's extension. "Gwen, schedule a meeting with the clothing-department heads for tomorrow at eleven. And make sure they know the meeting is mandatory." She hung up.

"I am impressed. When you get a bone in your teeth you don't let go, do you?"

"I'm here for a purpose and I don't intend to blow it this time," she told him. "Now, is there anything else to report or can it wait until tonight?"

Pete had the feeling he was being dismissed. "What's on for tonight?"

"You're coming over for dinner."

"What will Mom say?" he asked, wide-eyed.

"Probably a lot of things you won't want to hear," Brianne said candidly. "Are you up for it?"

He was tempted to tell her he was up for a hell of a lot, but opted to keep that thought to himself, for now. "For a free meal? Sure. Should I drag out my tux?"

"No, but it wouldn't hurt to wear a tie. If you don't have one, try our men's department. I'm sure Charles can find you a suitable one," she advised.

"Do I get a discount?"

"That's not how we make a profit here."

Pete grinned. Now this was the Brianne he'd come to know and desire.

"What time?"

"Drinks are at six," she instructed. "And believe me, my mother adheres to a strict timetable."

The moment Pete looked at Brianne, he knew he wasn't going to settle for a polite handshake to say goodbye. No, he wanted a hell of a lot more than holding her hand for a couple of seconds. He didn't stop to think that what he wanted was unprofessional and that if Rhyder knew he'd have a fit. Right now, Pete didn't care. Not when he could take advantage of the moment. Without a word of warning, he pulled her into his arms for a kiss guaranteed to smear that bright coral lipstick she wore. He noticed there was no protesting on her part as she leaned into his embrace. She was warm, smelled like heaven and felt even better. Her body seemed to flow against his, her lips parting to allow his tongue entrance. He couldn't remember ever tasting anything as good as she tasted. As far as he was concerned, he could stay like this for a long time. He felt frustration when she stepped back.

"You are a dangerous man, Pete Hackett," she murmured, her voice husky with the heat they'd just generated.

He held his hands out in his just-a-normal-kind-of-guy gesture. "I try. See ya tonight." He walked to the door, then paused before opening it. "I suppose you have a butler?"

Brianne smiled. "Haughty enough to serve under Her Majesty, the Queen."

He nodded. "Bet your mom loves him then." With a wave over his head, he left.

Gwen entered the office the moment Pete left. She held several sheets of paper in her hands.

"The meeting will be set up in the main conference room tomorrow morning," she announced. "Since it was available, I reserved it in your name. I thought you'd prefer that to your office."

"Great idea. Make sure there's coffee ready." Brianne looked over the papers the woman handed her.

"He's the detective you hired to find out who killed Mr. Matthews, isn't he?" she ventured.

Brianne nodded, then looked up from her reading. "I realize Mr. Hackett isn't the type of individual you're used to, but then, I don't think a majority of the population is used to someone like him." She wondered if Gwen could tell she had just been thoroughly kissed. She sure felt as if she had been! Her mouth fairly tingled with the memory, and she was grateful her hands weren't shaking.

"He looks like the kind of man you'd want on your side," Gwen confided.

"Yes, I'd say it was best to have him on your side," she agreed. "Anything else?"

"I was asked why you were setting up a meeting."

"What did you tell them?"

She straightened. "That if you wanted them to know, you would have said something, so they'll just have to wait until tomorrow to find out."

Brianne burst out laughing. "Good for you! We're going to show them that we aren't here purely for decorative purposes." She returned to her desk. "See if you can get copies of last year's women's-clothing orders. What I've seen out there is nice, but I can't believe we couldn't add some kickier lines."

"Kickier?"

She nodded. "Too much of the merchandise is geared for little old ladies who prefer black, navy and beige. I know those colors are classics, but there's no reason why we can't do some brightening up." She held out her arms to indicate her dress.

"Mrs. Roscoe has headed Misses Dresses for the last twenty years," Gwen whispered, as if the suggestion was sacrilege.

"And it looks it. I felt I was lucky to find the few items I did," Brianne answered. "Obviously, she doesn't look at the recent fashion magazines. If I have the title here, I intend to start using some of the power that goes with it. We're bringing those departments into the twentieth century if it kills us." She chuckled when she saw her secretary's concerned expression. "Don't worry. Nothing's going to happen to you. Your job is perfectly safe, Gwen. It's just time for some shaking up around here, and that's something I happen to be very good at," she proclaimed with great pride.

Gwen stared at her boss as if looking at a perfect stranger. "You sure have changed," she muttered as she walked out of the office.

Brianne leaned back in her chair, propping her legs, crossed at the ankle, on the desktop. "Oh, honey, you ain't seen nothin' yet," she murmured.

"ARE YOU GOING TO TELL ME what this is all about?" Trey demanded as Brianne drove out of the store's parking lot.

"Business."

He closed his eyes as she darted through the heavy midtown traffic with a careless ease he'd never known his sister to display. No wonder their mother was convinced Brianne was suffering from some kind of mental distress!

"Why did we have to leave the store to discuss business? Watch out!" He groaned when she raced up behind a truck, then deftly braked.

"Will you stop worrying?" she scolded, sliding between the truck and around a sedan. A driver in a Jaguar convertible honked and winked at her. She responded with a cheery wave. "And we won't be discussing business, we'll be conducting it. In a way."

He half turned in his seat to eye her suspiciously. "What do you mean, in a way?"

"I mean we are going to go shopping. Oh, there's the exit. I almost missed it." Deaf to horns blaring in their wake, she slipped across lanes with ease.

Trey looked at the sign over the building Brianne headed for. "When we have a perfectly good store of our own, why are you choosing to shop here?"

She perused the lot and found an empty space. Once she parked the car, she unfastened her seat belt and turned to her brother.

"I want to check out the competition," she stated. "We may have the longevity and reputation of quality merchandise, but that isn't bringing in the customers. If we want to increase sales, we need to start getting with the times. And that means throwing out a lot of old-fashioned ideas and bringing in a lot of new ones." She climbed out of the car and waited until he got out before arming the car alarm. "I'd like to see how they set up their departments, what they're selling. Things like that." She walked along briskly, even though she wore three-inch high heels.

Trey hurried to catch up with her. "What the hell do you think you know about merchandising?" he said fiercely, keeping his voice down.

"I know more than you think I know," she replied, seeming unconcerned that he'd just blatantly insulted her intelligence.

"How?" He wasn't about to stop there. He quickened his steps and pushed open the glass door for her.

She gifted him with a sunny smile. "You forget, my dear brother, that the first step in merchandising is consumerism, and if there's something I know how to do, it's shop." She breezed on past him before he had a chance to say a word.

Very good, my dear. You do realize you are only baffling him with a variety of words.

I know that, Mathias, Brianne answered silently. *But if that's what it takes, that's what I'll do.*

It was several hours before they left the mall. Brianne's mind was spinning with ideas, while Trey was loaded down with packages.

"I don't understand any of this," he grumbled, stashing bags in the BMW's trunk. "You throw out a perfectly good wardrobe you'd just purchased. All excellent classic styles that can go anywhere. Now, you're wearing all the colors of the rainbow.''

No wonder Brianne had such a boring wardrobe. She looked at classic. Not fun. "I've decided life is too short and I don't intend to be known as 'Best Dressed in the Boring Class,'" she said out loud. "Didn't you see the differences in there? How the departments were laid out? What they offered? I'd like to set up a junior department in our store." ·

"Kids?" He made a face, as if the idea was disagreeable.

"Today's kids are tomorrow's shoppers." She expertly backed out of the parking space and drove down the aisle, tapping the steering wheel with her fingertips. "You know, that would be a great slogan, wouldn't it?"

He merely groaned and rubbed his head.

"Trey, what's wrong?" She noticed his action. "You don't have a headache, do you? We have so much to discuss! I just know that with some changes we can turn Sinclairs into a store to be reckoned with!" Her voice rose with her enthusiasm.

He could only groan again. What had happened to his quiet, sane sister who never involved herself in store business and just enjoyed going in and pretending to work? The one who preferred dealing with charity events over anything to do with real work? All of a sudden she'd turned into a dynamo he felt he had no way of keeping up with. He winced when she turned on the radio to a rock-and-roll station. It was another change in her personality he couldn't fathom. She always used to listen to classical music.

"Oh, Mr. Hackett will be joining us for dinner tonight," Brianne announced.

Trey fumbled in his jacket pocket for his roll of antacid tablets. Life was taking some turns he wasn't sure he could navigate. What scared him even more was that it appeared Brianne was going to be able to take them with great ease.

Chapter Ten

Pete might have already known that Brianne came from old money, but the Sinclair house in South Pasadena merely confirmed it. House, hell. It was a mansion! Set back from the road and guarded by electronic gates, the stucco, three-story structure with its red-tiled roof was a tribute to Spanish architecture.

"Remington Steele would have felt right at home here," he muttered, climbing out of his Porsche. He tugged at his tie, which he was convinced was strangling him, and mounted the steps to the front door.

Within seconds of his pushing the doorbell, the large oak double doors opened to reveal a tall, cadaverous man dressed in a formal black suit, crisp white shirt and black tie.

Pete was glad he had borrowed a tie from Rhyder rather than opting for one from down at the local thrift shop. The last time he'd been in there, the quietest tie they'd offered had neon-colored fish on a bright blue background.

"Mr. Hackett." The man stated his name without making it a question as he stepped back to allow Pete to enter. "The family is already having their before-dinner drinks in the drawing room." He held out his hand for Pete's leather jacket and took it with a two-fingered grip, as if afraid it would contaminate his skin.

"Sounds good to me." Pete tried not to look too curious as he surveyed his surroundings while ambling along behind the butler.

The man opened double doors with the panache only a well-trained servant could display and announced, "Mr. Hackett."

Pete felt as if he had entered a play as he stepped inside the room—a drama filled with a great deal of tension. Olivia, elegant in a burgundy velvet dinner dress, was seated in her wheelchair, her back erect, as if a steel rod had been inserted along her spine. Pete wouldn't have been surprised to learn she'd had done just that so she would always have perfect posture. She had stopped near the couch, where Trey and Sheila were seated side by side. Brianne stood off to the right. While two of the players looked edgy, one was remarkably calm and one showed no expression at all.

Brianne turned and walked toward Pete. "Mr. Hackett, how nice of you to join us." She greeted him with her hands outstretched.

Pete nodded dumbly, remembering just in time to take her hands so he wouldn't look like an idiot. He only had to glance at her to forget he was about to walk into a nest of vipers, with Olivia Sinclair the head terminator. How had Brianne been born into such a cold family? Of course, he only had to look at her to warm right up.

She was wearing black. The color may have been conservative, but the outfit definitely wasn't. Her hip-length vest bared her arms and skimmed her body, showing nothing, yet hinting at more than enough. It was her pants that caught his attention. They were fashioned of fabric sheer enough for a harem dancer. Every line of her spectacular long legs was revealed by the filmy garment, the hems of which just brushed her black, strappy, high-heeled sandals. Red-tipped toes peeked through her black stockings. Her hair flowed in tousled waves to her shoulders, looking as if she had just gotten out of bed, and black-beaded earrings dangled. Another thought came to Pete as he tried not to drool. But dammit, those red, glossy lips were made for kissing!

"Mother, I'm sure you remember Pete Hackett." Brianne kept hold of his hand in her cool fingers as she led him across the room.

Olivia's expression wasn't as welcoming. "Mr. Hackett," she said coolly, holding out her hand.

Pete took it, wryly wondering if he was supposed to bow and kiss it. He settled for a handshake and dropped it. Trey nodded as Brianne said his name, and Sheila smiled and offered her hand. "I understand you were with the police department, Mr. Hackett," she said brightly as the butler presented him with a drink.

Pete sipped the liquid cautiously, then relaxed when he realized it was very good Scotch whiskey.

"Yes, ma'am, for about ten years."

"He was a detective with many citations and commendations to his credit," Brianne interjected.

Pete wondered how she knew that, then realized all it would take was a few phone calls and not even all that much pull. He didn't have to turn his head to know Brianne was close by. He could smell the seductive scent of her perfume and sense her presence.

"I will be honest with you, Mr. Hackett," Olivia began without preamble.

This should be something to hear. I bet you've never been honest one day in your life, lady, he thought cynically, though he kept a bland expression.

"We don't require your services. Michael's death was unfortunate, but there is nothing we can do about it." Olivia took a tiny sip of her wine. "But we can ensure this doesn't get out of hand by having Brianne come to her senses and do what our family attorney recommends."

Pete put his drink down on the table beside him.

"Your family attorney recommends that your daughter admit she's one can minus a six-pack. And then spend some time at one of those resorts that offer peace and quiet, heavy-duty tranquilizers, padded rooms if necessary, and hey, if that doesn't work, there's always a nice little designer straitjacket in just her size," Pete said bluntly. "Oh, right, anyone who didn't kill someone would jump to admit she did it under duress just so she can be carted off for a nice, long, relaxing rest." His eyes turned a deep, stormy gray. "What the hell kind of mother are you, anyway?"

Olivia straightened in her chair. "I am the best mother she could have," she stated. "Brianne has had the best upbringing a girl could ask for, and I will do everything necessary to keep her happy."

Including get you out of her life. The thought bounced around in Pete's head. Except the puzzling thing was he was positive the voice wasn't his.

"Do you honestly believe she didn't kill Michael Matthews?" he demanded.

Her gaze didn't waver. "Of course, I do. That is the only reason you were allowed in this house."

"And so you could again tell me my services were no longer required," he guessed. The faint flutter of her eyelashes told him he had hit it right on the nose.

"Excuse me?" Brianne stepped between them, waving her hands in front of her. "You're doing it again. You're speaking about me as if I wasn't here. Guess what? I am here and I've taken charge of my life. Which means I'm paying Pete and Rhyder's fees."

Olivia sniffed, as if a terrible odor had reached her nose. "Rhyder Carson is a man with no scruples. He's no better than those ambulance chasers you hear about. He's only taking your case because it guarantees him getting his name in the paper again. Something he enjoys seeing, since it means he'll draw more clients gullible enough to pay for his services."

Pete tamped down the anger that rose in his chest. He hadn't expected Olivia to welcome him with open arms. He'd expected her to take a few well-mannered potshots at him, but she was going beyond that. She was moving in for the kill. And before he'd even had a chance to have dinner, no less!

"Rhyder Carson was in the top ten of his class at Harvard," he said slowly. "*Law Review,* Moot Court, clerk to a Supreme Court judge—you name it, he did it. He chose criminal law because he felt there were a lot of innocent people out there who weren't getting a fair shake and he was determined to make sure they got one. He chooses his clients carefully. Not because he's looking for an easy win, but because he doesn't want to put a truly guilty person back on the streets. He relies heavily on his instincts, and to date, they haven't let him down." He refused to look away from the woman's intimidating stare.

Her smile didn't hold one ounce of humor. "Brianne hasn't been herself since the unfortunate incident. It's up to her family to be with her and help her during this trying time. Your assistance appears to be more harmful with your intrusion into our private lives. I do not appreciate hearing that my friends have been bothered with your questions."

"Did your friends tell you that the cops were there one step ahead of me?" he asked her. "And their questions were a hell of a lot more personal than any I came up with."

The expression on her face tightened until it resembled a cold, marble mask. "All Brianne had to do was agree to Joshua's suggestion and none of this would have happened."

"The store cannot afford any negative publicity, Mr. Hackett. My sister's case is drawing just that." Trey chimed in, only to shrink back from his mother's warning glare.

Pete noticed that during Olivia's share of their illuminating conversation, Brianne remained quiet. But something in her stance told him she was alert to all that was going on. He bristled, furious that they were again discussing her as if she wasn't there, and furious that she wasn't contributing to the conversation.

Still, he told himself, maybe it was better she stayed out of it right now. Talking to and observing her mother was showing him a lot about the woman.

His brow wrinkled as he played back the conversation in his head. "Why do you always refer to Brianne by name?" he asked suddenly. "You never call her your daughter. Why?"

Olivia turned her head, staring at Brianne. Most people would have been unsettled by that steady gaze, but the younger woman merely returned it with one of her own.

"Perhaps it has something to do with her not being my daughter," Olivia said, ignoring Trey's automatic protest. "I don't know who she is, but she most certainly is not Brianne Sinclair."

Brianne didn't react to her mother's announcement, but Pete found himself with a bad taste in his mouth and no desire to remain there another minute. "I normally am not this rude, but I feel I have a good reason this time." He stood up. "Com'on, Brianne, let's get out of here." Keeping his eyes fastened on Olivia—the best advice he'd ever got was never to turn his back on the enemy—he held out his hand. She stepped over and took it, her fingers cool against his. He noticed Olivia glance at their clasped hands, and her eyes blazed with something he couldn't read. He'd bet his Porsche she knew more about that night than she was willing to admit. "I must say you give a whole new meaning to the word *family*. Thanks for the drink. It's been interesting." He walked out, still hanging on to Brianne's hand.

She looked over her shoulder. "Don't wait up for me."

He muttered under his breath as the butler brought him his jacket and a coat for Brianne. Pete barely let her put on her coat before he grabbed hold of her hand again and practically dragged her outside to his car. He remembered his manners in time to assist her into the passenger seat before walking around to the driver's side. She barely had her seat belt fastened before he took off.

She remained silent as he drove off the property. Every once in a while he muttered something indistinguishable under his breath and pounded the steering wheel with his fist.

"How can you live in that mausoleum?" he asked suddenly as he turned onto the freeway. Luckily, the traffic was light, so he could increase his speed. "I have never met a more self-serving, cold-mannered..." He stopped, running out of descriptions.

"They make the Addams Family seem normal, don't they?" Brianne looked out the car window. "I hope you realize you're going to have to feed me now."

He gave her a quick look. "You're dressed a little too formal for McDonalds."

"I'd just give them a thrill."

"Why does your mother hate you so much?"

He was out of luck if he expected a gasp of pain at his question. "I don't think she likes anyone very much," Brianne answered. "She's concentrating on me right now because of the unwanted publicity Michael's death has brought the family."

"And that's why she's practically disowning you?"

She was still looking out the window, so he couldn't see her reaction to his question. "No, that's something entirely different." She turned her head and watched him with a pensive expression on her face. "No matter what you think about her, she's a very perceptive woman. She has a way of ferreting out secrets."

"Yours?" He wasn't about to believe she was guilty of murder. It didn't jive. Yet everything he'd learned about her so far didn't mesh. Who was the real Brianne Sinclair?

The real Brianne Sinclair is the one before you. You should believe in her.

Pete shook his head as if trying to dislodge the thought that sounded so loud and clear in his head.

"I know a place," he said. "It's out of the way. There's no atmosphere and no wine list, but the food's good."

"That's fine."

They were both silent the rest of the way. Pete kept asking himself why he was going to so much trouble for one client. He never had before. Sure, it could be because she had a great pair of legs and a body to go with it. Or a pair of eyes that seemed to see all the way to his soul.

That was what threw him for a loop—the way she looked at him, as if she had known him for years. Yet the more he was with her, the more he felt as if there had once been something between them.

The restaurant was built on the beach on the outskirts of Malibu. The exterior was plain and looked more like a beach shack.

"How can you say there's no atmosphere?" Brianne commented as they sat at a table on the deck overlooking the sand. "It looks like the perfect place for people on the run." She traced her finger around the rim of the water glass.

"Like you?" Pete asked.

When the waitress approached them for their drink order, Pete asked for a beer and Brianne requested club soda.

"I think I'm going to need my wits about me tonight," she explained with a smile.

When their drinks arrived, Pete held up his glass. "No business talk," he announced by way of a toast.

Brianne picked up hers and clinked it against his. "Sounds fair, but we both know we won't be able to stay away from it."

The candle on the table flickered in the evening breeze, sending shadows across her face.

For a moment, Pete felt as if he was looking at an entirely different person. Black glossy waves instead of ash blond. Sparkling dark eyes instead of dreamy green. Sharp features instead of delicate cheekbones.

Memories prodded him as he stared at the woman seated across from him. Yet, for just a moment he could have sworn another figure stood just behind her, one with dark hair instead of light. He couldn't even blame his vision on the drink, since he didn't have enough alcohol in him to cause it!

"Allie," he muttered, unthinking. He had lowered his head to stare at the table, so he missed the tremble of her lips.

She coughed. "Allie's the friend who was killed?" she whispered.

He nodded. "Someone who didn't deserve to die the way she did. I've been doing a little nosing around to find out about her murder."

"Yes," she said in a husky voice.

Pete nodded. He felt a choking sensation deep in his throat.

"Did you love her?"

He was silent for a long time. "You know, we never had a chance to find out."

Brianne had to turn away before she broke down in tears. *I have to tell him!* she screamed silently. *I have to tell him who I really am.*

And do you think he'd believe you?

He will if I give him enough proof.

Peter is a very logical man. What you are proposing to tell him is not logical.

She wished she had a solid human being to lash out at instead of what felt like a wisp of smoke in her head.

Thank you very much, Mr. Spock, she thought sarcastically. *You are not being any help here.*

I'm here to help you, not assist you in making a fool of yourself.

"Those thoughts you're having must be heavy-duty," Pete said quietly.

Brianne managed a smile. "Yes, I guess they are." Instead of indulging his curiosity, she opened the menu. "Um, it all looks good," she said brightly. "Be prepared for a big bill, Hackett. I'm starving."

As she intently studied the menu, she was aware of his gaze on her. She remembered seeing that look on his face before—every time he thought about something that puzzled him. Except this time the problem bothering him wasn't a what, but a who, and she began to worry that he wasn't going to let go until he figured things out to his satisfaction. Amusement tickled the edge of her mind. She wondered what he would say when she told him that Allie wasn't dead...in the strict sense of the word.

"LET'S WALK ON THE BEACH," Brianne suggested as they lingered over after-dinner coffee. She had already enjoyed her dessert of chocolate mousse.

He cocked an eyebrow. "You're not exactly dressed for it."

"Don't worry about me," she exclaimed.

Pete paid the bill and they walked around the building to the wooden stairs leading down to the beach. When they reached the sand, Brianne placed her hand on his shoulder for balance as she slipped off her shoes. She grimaced when she realized her pant hems dragged in the sand.

"Turn around," she ordered. She waited until he obeyed, then quickly unfastened the pants and slid them and her thigh-high, sheer black stockings down her legs. "All right, you can turn around now."

Pete exhaled in a short whistle as he looked at the long expanse of bare leg. Then, without a word, he took her stockings and pants, rolled them up in a ball and put them in his jacket pocket. Since she had left her coat in the car, she only had her vest, which covered just enough to insure she wouldn't be arrested.

"You like to live on the edge, don't you?" he asked, as Brianne led the way down to the water's edge. She dipped her toes in the foaming surf, then squealed as the cold water ran over her feet.

"I like to know I'm alive." She broke free and danced ahead of him, walking backward so she could face him. That particular stretch of beach was lit by lamps from the restaurant and parking lot above them. The orange light, meant to aid drivers during foggy days and nights, sent an eerie glow that looked as if it had come from another world across her up-turned face. "I can't afford to let anything pass me by anymore. I want to experience everything!" She stretched her arms above her head. "I can't afford to miss out on anything!"

"Considering your family's net worth, I don't think you have to worry about that," Pete said dryly.

Brianne shook her head. The smile touching her lips was bittersweet. "Did you ever believe in that phrase about things not being what they appear to be?" she asked.

"Every day I was on the force."

This isn't the time, Brianne. If you tell him now, you will lose him. Oh, you won't lose Peter Hackett the private investigator. His scruples will ensure that he'll help you. But you will have lost the man and that is the one thing you know you do not want to lose.

She gave no indication a conversation was going on in her head. Instead she walked forward, graceful even on the uneven sand. She looped her arms around his neck and brought his face down to hers. The scent of her perfume surrounded him like a silken cloud, inspiring erotic fantasies, while the feel of her body against his left him hungry for the sensation of bare skin against skin. Their kiss was soft as a kitten's fur, the kind of kiss that inspires poetry. In Pete, it also inspired a lot of lusty thoughts.

"Pete," she whispered, once she drew back.

"Yes." He found he had to whisper, too, so as not to jar the spell between them.

"Pete, why don't you take me to your apartment?" she asked huskily.

Talk about temptation! She was in his arms, asking him to take her to his place, and he knew it wasn't for a cup of coffee! Still, he had to keep a sensible head right about now. Even if the rest of him didn't agree.

"I'm not so sure that's a good idea."

Brianne pressed feathery kisses along his jawline and around his mouth. "Oh, I think it's a wonderful idea," she murmured, punctuating each word with another breathy kiss. "Because for what I have planned, we could be arrested if we remain much longer on the beach. And I'm sure you'd hate the idea of anyone you know either arresting you or finding out you were arrested on the beach for participating in lewd activities." The tip of her tongue appeared, feathering its way across his bottom lip as her hips nudged his. "After all, what fun could we have spending the night in jail? All those hours in separate cells wouldn't be all that enjoyable, would it?"

He was finding it harder to breathe. "Yeah." It was amazing he could even get out that one word without choking.

"So?" She stepped back and cocked her head to one side as she waited for his answer.

Pete found himself doing a lot of things around Brianne he didn't normally do. He grasped her around the waist and swung her in a circle, enjoying the sound of her laughter ringing out over the surf pounding on the rocks a short distance away.

"God help me, but I guess I'm about to show you the messiest apartment in the county."

Chapter Eleven

Pete was positive he broke just about every speed law in the book getting back to his apartment. He parked his car and assisted Brianne out with great care.

"I, ah, I should warn you I'm not the world's best housekeeper," he mumbled, frantically trying to remember if he'd put clean sheets on the bed that week. He guided her up the stairs to the third floor as he wondered if his dirty clothes had ended up in the hamper or were still strewn around the bedroom. Maybe also the living room. And perhaps the kitchen.

"I promise not to use the white-glove test on the furniture," she assured him, staying close to him.

Pete fumbled with the door key, swallowing the curse that almost left his lips. He couldn't believe himself! It wasn't as if he was a virgin. As if he'd never had a woman in his apartment before. Except none of them had been Brianne, and he wanted everything to be right with her.

"Pete." Her fingers were cool against his nape when she rested them against his skin.

He grasped her fingers and brought them around to his mouth as he pushed the door open and pulled her along with him.

The only light burning was the one over the stove in the kitchen. He moved to flip on a lamp, but she stopped him.

"You don't have to give me a tour right away. Let's keep the lights off. I'd like us to do this by touch," she whispered, moving until her body nestled against his. "What better way for us to find out everything about each other?"

She barely had the words out before his mouth covered hers. There was no way he was going to let her have all the control!

Brianne slipped her hands under his jacket, yanking it off as he was busy pushing off her coat and unbuttoning her vest.

Pete breathed in sharply as her skin gleamed like a pearl in the darkness. With her black lacy bra and the sheer pants, which she'd slipped on again before they left the beach, she looked even more the part of a harem dancer. She was all his dreams come true in one sexy package.

"If I die tonight, I will die a happy man," he said simply, still unable to stop himself from staring.

Her face lit up in pleasure at his reaction. "Oh Pete, you may die, but it will only be a little death. The kind you'll bounce back from, I guarantee it," she whispered.

He shucked his shirt, almost strangling himself with his tie, as they made their way to the bedroom. He breathed a sigh of relief to find the quilt pulled up over the bed, which meant he had put clean sheets on that morning. It was the only time he remembered to pull the quilt up!

Brianne made sexy little movements with her hips as she unfastened his belt and pants.

"Pete!" she exhaled his name and a breath of warm air tickled his neck.

"What?"

"Um, nothing, just Pete." She nibbled her way across his jaw. "I like saying your name."

He was busying finding the fastener to her bra and unhooking it. The lace cups fell to each side, baring her breasts to his greedy gaze. With his vision accustomed to the darkness, he felt he could see her lush shape, but he wished to see the rich color of her nipples. He settled for touch. She quivered and gasped when his hand covered her breast, his thumb rubbing against her erect nipple in an arousing circular motion. Soon it wasn't enough and he dipped his head to taste her.

Brianne's own head fell back, her eyes closed against the sheer ecstasy flowing through her body as her nipple was enclosed by the wet heat of his mouth. Lightning streaked through her as he suckled. She gripped his shoulders, afraid she would fall to the floor if she didn't hold on to him. She almost breathed a sigh of relief when she felt the cool fabric of his quilt under her back. But the sensation was instantly superceded by the searing heat of his body against hers.

Brief pictures flashed against her closed eyelids. Of Whit, who was always more involved with his own pleasure than hers. Even of Michael, who'd been clearly of the old school and thought ladies didn't enjoy sex or actively participate. This was different. Pete murmured dark, earthy words in her ear, praising her body, encouraging her and doing things to her that brought a smile to her lips, even as he kissed her.

Her filmy pants were stripped off at a leisurely pace as he placed kisses along her ankle and behind her knee. She was glad she hadn't bothered with her stockings when they left the beach. When his lips reached the crease at her upper thigh she thought she would surely die. A wild thought suddenly followed that one and she almost laughed. How could she die when she already had?

He slid the narrow, lace-banded bikini panties off last. When they reached her ankles, she blindly kicked them free. She was so eager to feel all of him against her, she almost tore off his briefs, tossing them to one side.

"Are we taking this slow and sexy or fast and wild?" Pete muttered against her lips.

"You can't expect me to answer any questions right now!" Brianne wailed, as his fingers combed the silky blond patch of hair, one finger curving downward to unerringly find that sensitive spot. Her hips moved under his caress. "I can't think!"

He chuckled, rubbing his mouth against her temple. "Who said anything about thinking?"

She clung to him. "Just love me, Pete. Love me."

She wasn't sure which meaning of the word she intended. Only that he stop the sensual torture he'd begun. Except he wasn't about to stop.

"Not just yet," he murmured, one leg edging between hers and making room for his hips. "I've been thinking about you for a long time, Bri. Let's see how far we can get before we both go up in flames."

If she could have uttered one coherent word she would have told him she was already feeling like a major forest fire. But then, something reminded her that there was no reason why she couldn't fight his fire with a torch of her own.

She reached down and found his erection, encircling it with her fingers. He felt hot and silky to the touch, with a hint of steel beneath. She smiled as he groaned when she did some stroking of her own.

"Fair's fair," she whispered, sliding her curved fingers up and down slowly while her other hand moved up and down his side, and her nails drew loving pictures on his skin. She raised her head, using the tip of her tongue against his nipple, causing it to harden into a small pebble.

She wished she had asked to have the lights on, so she could see his face. With the curtains drawn in his bedroom, the light was minimal and she could only see his shadowy outline above her. Only imagine the expression on his face. Still, she could feel his reactions. Hear his voice as he told her how she made him feel as he touched her. As she touched him.

He hadn't even entered her and she already felt as if he was making soul-stealing love to her. Tears filled her eyes, but she blinked them away before they could fall.

"Pete," she whispered, lightly scratching him with her nails.

He mumbled a curse as he reached over her and pulled open the nightstand drawer. He rummaged through the contents until he found a foil packet. She took it from him and opened it, sheathing him with her gentle touch.

Pete flexed his hips, pushing forward slowly, allowing them both to savor the moment. He laced his fingers through hers, pressing her hands back down on the pillow on either side of her head as he surged forward.

Brianne couldn't keep her gaze off his face. She was positive she could see the fierce desire etched on his features. His stormy eyes flashed lightning bolts as he looked down on her. Then she couldn't see anything as he dropped his head and began kissing her hungrily. His ferocity didn't frighten her, because she felt the same potent emotions running through her veins.

At that moment, she knew if something happened and she was gone tomorrow, she wouldn't regret it because she would always have this one night with Pete.

She cried out in frenzied pleasure as he moved his hips against hers, faster and faster until they were both caught up in the firestorm raging about them.

Brianne wasn't afraid of the flames that threatened to consume them. She knew she wasn't alone as long as Pete held her tightly in his arms. She cried out his name when she felt herself fall into the fiery volcano, only to hear him say "Brianne," at the same time with the exact same awe she felt.

Pete was gasping for air as he rolled to one side. He kept his arms around her and nestled her against his side.

She rested her cheek in the hollow of his shoulder and idly combed her fingers through the damp hair matting his chest. She breathed in the warm, musky scent of his skin, which held a hint of her own scent.

She smiled as she thought of the two blending together so well.

"So," she murmured, as she forced air back into her lungs, "when exactly does all the fun you've been promising begin?"

She could hear his rumbling laughter as it worked its way up his chest and throat. He rolled her over until she was flat on her back, then loomed over her in what might look like a menacing posture to some. But she already knew what a pussycat Pete Hackett really was.

"Princess, if I had one ounce of strength left, I'd take you up on that challenge."

She smiled. "Funny, I'd say you had no problem taking me up a few minutes ago."

PETE COULDN'T REMEMBER the last time he'd slept so well or so deeply. Maybe it had something to do with the soft bundle of femininity in his arms, but he wasn't about to question it. All he knew was that sleeping with Brianne next to him was about as close to heaven as he could ever hope to get.

He wasn't sure what woke him first—a woman's voice softly humming a tune or the scent of coffee teasing his nostrils. He rolled over onto his back and opened his eyes.

"It's about time you decided to rejoin the land of the living."

He blinked several times to better focus on the picture in front of him. The early morning light showed Brianne, wearing his shirt with the sleeves rolled up to her elbows, sitting cross-legged on the end of the bed.

A mug of coffee was cradled in her hands. The ends of her hair were damp.

"I have taken a shower, clattered around your basically empty kitchen, made coffee and was thinking of opening the curtains next," she announced. "Just to see if you were still alive."

Pete leaned forward and took the mug out of her hands. He sipped cautiously, then eagerly as he realized it was fixed the way he liked it—black and strong enough to float a battleship.

"You know how to make coffee," he murmured, inhaling the aromatic steam with great appreciation.

"Don't be so surprised, big guy." She shot him a sly glance under the cover of lowered lashes. "There's a lot of things I know how to do."

He grinned, looking like a man who'd had a wonderful night of fantastic sex. "Yeah, I could tell."

Brianne pretended to look miffed, but the devilment in her eyes took over. She leaned forward and crept across the length of the bed with feline grace, her back arched. She uttered a few feral growls for effect as she made her way up his body. "If you aren't nice to me, you might not get any more—" she pursed her lips "—coffee."

Pete was positive there wasn't a speck of energy left in his body after last night. By rights, he should be exhausted. But when he saw the enticing way his shirtfront gaped away from her chest, revealing creamy breasts with dusky pink nipples already peaked, he realized he was more than ready. He set the mug on the nightstand and pulled open the drawer.

"Are you threatening to withhold—" he paused as she settled herself on his lap with the sheet between them "—more coffee?"

Her lips were slightly swollen from their kisses and moist as she lowered her face to his. She gave a wiggle and the sheet slid downward.

"They say caffeine is an excellent restorative," she murmured, leisurely unbuttoning the shirt until it fell open.

He doubted he could ever get his fill of her. "Yeah."

Brianne continued smiling as she wiggled a bit more. "Let's find out, shall we?"

SHE WAS STILL SMILING when Pete dropped her off at her door with a kiss that rapidly threatened to get out of hand.

"Rhyder's office this afternoon," he murmured.

She nodded. Her hand rested lightly on his thigh, gently kneading upward. "I'll meet you there."

"Dinner?"

She nodded. "Let's forgo the before-dinner drinks this time."

He chuckled. "Good idea."

With one last kiss, Brianne got out the car and ran up the steps. She held her breath as she crept upstairs to her room. Relieved she didn't run into anyone, she washed her hair, pulling the damp strands back in an intricate braid. After applying her makeup, she studied the contents of her closet, in search of a dress appropriate for the way she felt that day.

The one she chose was black, but sported multicolored triangle inserts along the hem of the fitted garment. She wore a short chain necklace dotted with the same-color beads as the inserts. She stood in front of the mirror, admiring her reflection.

I must say you look remarkably refreshed considering the exertions of last night.

"Mathias?" She panicked. "Did you peek?"

Naturally not. Once I realized what the two of you were up to, I went off elsewhere. Are you sure it was a good idea?

Her smile threatened to split her face. "Oh yes, it was a wonderful idea." She swung around in a circle.

Does that mean you've decided not to tell him your hopelessly illogical story?

Brianne grimaced. "I still feel I should tell him, but I'm afraid if I do, he's not going to understand."

Amazing, Brianne. Isn't that the same thing I told you?

"Not at all," she said haughtily.

I only hope you're prepared for the consequences.

"There won't be any." Humming under her breath, she left her room and practically danced down the stairs.

"I see you've decided to return home."

Brianne made a face before turning around with a bright smile firmly pasted on her lips. "Good morning, Mother. Did you sleep well?"

Olivia didn't return her smile. "Obviously better than you did. I do hope you took precautions. A man like him has no morals."

Brianne's fingers flexed. "That was totally uncalled for. Pete Hackett is one of the finest men I've ever met."

"Yes, and you wouldn't have met him if it hadn't been for Michael's death." There was the faintest flicker of emotion in her eyes.

"You know something," Brianne whispered. "You know something about that night."

Olivia raised her chin to its usual imperious level. "What I know is that you are not my daughter. I don't know what occurred or how it happened, but you are not the Brianne I brought into this world," she said in a low voice. "Why should I bother to protect a fraud?" She turned her wheelchair around and glided silently toward the elevator.

Brianne itched to go after her and demand an explanation. But deep down, she feared an all-out confrontation with the older woman. What if she found a way to convince others Brianne was a fake? Even worse, what if she found a way to make sure Brianne spent a long time in one of those hospitals where they dispensed tranquilizers like candy? The thought made her go cold inside. She suddenly had the need to get out of the house as fast as possible. At that moment, she didn't care if she ever returned.

BRIANNE GRABBED her breakfast at a fast-food drive through and walked into her office well ahead of everyone else. She sat down with a pad and pen, wrote rapidly and left her notes on Gwen's desk to be typed up.

"Ms. Sinclair?" Gwen popped her head in the doorway half an hour later.

"One and the same." Brianne waved her pen over her head.

The young woman looked worried. "I'll make the coffee right away."

"Don't worry, I already made it." A smile touched her lips as she thought of the pot of coffee she'd made just after dawn. She couldn't remember ever having a cup that tasted so good. "Would you please type up the notes I left on your desk and make enough copies for everyone at the meeting?"

"Right away."

As the meeting time grew closer, butterflies started assaulting her stomach and doubts made their existence loud and clear. What did she know about merchandising other than as a consumer? She hadn't gone to college except for taking a few night courses, and those were self-help classes.

You're not going to throw up or something equally disgusting, are you?

Brianne decided she was beginning to hate that irritating voice. "No, I'm not," she retorted, but softly, so Gwen wouldn't overhear her. She took several deep breaths to calm her racing pulse and stepped out of her office.

She halted near Gwen's desk. The younger woman gathered up a stack of folders and followed her down the hallway.

Brianne breathed a silent sigh of relief when Mathias directed her to the proper door. She would have hated to open someone's office door accidentally. When she opened it, she found the chairs around the conference table filled. Several sets of eyes were curious, other gazes suspicious. She smiled at each one, aware she had her work cut out for her.

"Good morning," she said in greeting.

"We usually have our meetings the first of the month, Ms. Sinclair," Mrs. Roscoe stated. "You know you're always more than welcome to sit in on them."

Yes, and I bet you were relieved I never showed up, Brianne thought to herself as she smiled at the woman. "Thank you," she said out loud. "But I felt this was important enough to call a special meeting." She nodded to Gwen, who passed out a folder to each person. "My brother and I visited two of our competitors yesterday. I was curious to see how they set up their departments, and what I found puts ours to shame."

Mrs. Roscoe almost shot out of her chair. "We have an excellent reputation in this county. No store can equal what we have."

"We have an excellent reputation for the silver-haired set," Brianne said candidly. "We have very little to offer the younger crowd."

"Why should we worry about a market we haven't entered before?" Louise Rawlins, the sportswear manager, asked. "We've been **do**ing very well without them."

"No, we haven't done well," Brianne flatly stated. "Sales have slowly but steadily dropped in the past ten years." She gestured toward some figures she'd pulled together that morning. "No red-blooded teenager is going to want to shop in a store her grandmother frequents. In order for us to attract their business, and keep it, we need to update our present departments and find space for a junior division."

"And just where do you propose to put a junior department?" Mrs. Roscoe made the last two words sound like an abomination.

Brianne knew this was where the battle would begin, but she felt fully prepared to fight it. "By dispensing with the fur salon and that far corner in your department."

The gray-haired woman puffed out her chest. "I have need for every inch of space in my department."

"Not if you do a little reorganizing. You'd still have more than enough space for display purposes."

"What do you suggest we do? Cram merchandise together, leaving customers little room to walk?" Louise demanded.

Brianne shook her head. "Not at all. Every department has lines that don't sell even when they're marked way down. And with so many people disliking the idea of wearing real fur, I believe we should do our part in closing the fur salon."

Greg Ferris, menswear manager, seemed to be studying the figures she'd compiled carefully. "Are you planning this expansion to cater to both sexes?" he asked, still looking as skeptical as the others.

Brianne shook her head. "I believe we have a better chance at attracting girls than boys," she replied. "Perhaps we should offer teen makeovers in the beginning. Plan some fashion shows. What I would really like is to find a fairly new designer who creates clothing that would appeal to teen girls and carry that line on an exclusive basis."

"It would bring the quality of the store down to the common level." Mrs. Roscoe sniffed with disdain.

"If done correctly, sales and quality would be up," she argued, leaning forward as she pressed home her points. "All the departments could use a coat of paint. Perhaps carpeting and new furniture. After visiting those other stores, about the only thing I could see that we have better is our dressing rooms. Not one of the fitting rooms I checked out had lighting that made a woman feel attractive, was roomy or had decent mirrors."

"It's nice to know we excel in something," Mrs. Roscoe muttered darkly.

Brianne chose to ignore the woman's remark instead of calling her on it.

"Since you're talking about eradicating my department, what do you expect to do with me?" Constance Shaw, the fur salon manager, asked in an icy voice.

Brianne hid her dismay. This was the one thing she was afraid of. Constance had been with Sinclairs even longer than Mrs. Roscoe. The woman had started in the accessories department in the early fifties, selling gloves and hats, and had worked her way up from there. She had been in charge of the fur salon for the past twelve years. Brianne knew from her personnel records that she would be eligible for retirement in two years, and gathered from her attitude that she wasn't about to retire early, even if they offered her a generous retirement package.

"We're not talking about throwing you out on the street, Mrs. Shaw," she explained with her brightest smile.

But the woman wasn't willing to hear any of it. She stood up. "Your mother will not allow this." She dismissed Brianne's research with a contemptuous flick of her finger against the folder.

Brianne refused to back down. "My mother is no longer in charge here."

Constance offered a chilly smile. "No, but your brother is and he won't allow it, either."

"I've already discussed this with my brother and he agrees with me," she said quietly.

"I don't believe you!"

Brianne settled back in her chair as if she had nothing to worry about. Except that when she'd broached her idea to Trey, he had warned her she would have to battle Constance. He was in complete fear of the woman! "That's your choice. But you have to remember that Sinclairs has remained behind while the world moved ahead. We can't afford to do that any longer."

The older woman stared at her for several moments. "Tell me something. If anyone disagrees with you, will you just shoot him?"

Shocked murmurs filled the room as her blatant insult sank in. Brianne first thought about going for the woman's throat, then decided against it. After all, while Allie would definitely gouge her eyes out, Brianne wouldn't.

"That remark is beneath you, Constance." She deliberately used her first name.

Constance's cheeks were bright red as she left the room, but her head was held high. Brianne had a pretty good idea that she was heading for Trey's office, and she only hoped her brother would back her up. She looked around the table and noticed that a majority of the others were embarrassed for her. She was glad to see they all didn't agree with Constance.

A tiny part of her jumped up and down with glee for not going for Constance's throat. Another part reminded her she still had Trey to worry about.

"Anyone have anything else to say or can we get on with the meeting?" she asked in a calm voice that belied the Mexican jumping beans in her stomach.

"Will you also be including a junior shoe section and jewelry counter or will they be a part of the standard departments?" someone else asked.

Brianne felt like bursting into song. "I don't know about you, but I thought we'd put it all together so they can coordinate everything there." She went on, now inspired to share her ideas. She felt as if she just might be able to make her mark after all.

Chapter Twelve

Brianne was walking on air. They liked her ideas! They were even enthusiastic enough to suggest a few of their own. She felt powerful. She felt as if she could move mountains.

She entered Rhyder's office building with the assurance of a woman who knew who she was. In a way. Humming under her breath, she punched the elevator button.

"Tell me something, is this the same woman who crawled out of my bed this morning?"

Brianne didn't bother turning around to identify the voice. She already recognized it. She continued staring straight ahead at the closed elevator doors. "No, this is not the sex kitten you cavorted with almost all night. This is the dominant force behind all the radical changes in Sinclairs Department Stores."

Pete's fingers briefly touched the small of her back. "Dominant, huh?" he murmured out of the corner of his mouth. "Sounds a little kinky, but I could give it a try. Do you wear black leather pants, spike heels and carry a whip?"

She had to force herself not to smile or look at him. "Only for very special people. Do you consider yourself special?"

"About as special as a guy can be. I'd really like to see you in that black leather."

Brianne found herself enjoying their word play. "I'm sure something can be arranged."

With a soft *ping,* the doors slid open. Still without looking at Pete, Brianne stepped inside the elevator. As she turned to face the doors, Pete stepped in as well and they both saw a man in his late fifties staring at them, a mixture of shock and fascination on his face.

"I'll just wait for the next car," he told them with a nervous smile.

Luckily, the doors slid shut right then, because the moment they closed, Brianne collapsed against the wall. Her body shook with her laughter. "I wonder how long he was standing there," she gasped.

Pete's grin was positively wicked. "The entire time."

Her eyes widened. A tiny whimper worked its way up her throat. "You mean he heard *everything?*"

He nodded, still grinning. "Believe me, it was obvious he didn't mind eavesdropping on our conversation. In fact, I think we made his day."

She buried her face in her hands. If there had been a hole in the floor she gladly would have crawled into it. "And we said all those things, too. What must he think of us?"

"Gauging by his interest, and the fact he nearly suffered whiplash leaning closer to hear everything, I'd say he thought we were pretty hot stuff."

Brianne continued groaning. She could feel the heat stealing across her cheeks and knew her face was bright red. She was never so grateful as when the elevator slid to a halt and the doors opened.

"Saved by the bell," he whispered, following her out of the elevator. "For now."

"Is that a promise or threat?"

"Definitely a promise."

She walked down the hallway toward Rhyder's office door. "I'll be looking forward to it."

Pete ambled on behind, entranced at the way her slender body swayed under the black linen dress. "So will I," he murmured.

Rhyder was standing at his secretary's desk when the couple entered. He looked from one to the other with the sharp gaze he was known for. One eyebrow cocked upward. He knew something had happened between them since the last meeting and he was pretty sure what that was.

Dressed in a white shirt with the sleeves rolled up to the elbow, his tie loosened at the neck and charcoal dress slacks due to a morning spent in court, he looked devastating. Brianne couldn't imagine any woman resisting his masculine charm. So why was it that looking at the rumpled Pete in his jeans, chambray shirt and ever-present leather jacket sent her heart racing, while it thumped at a normal rate when she looked at Rhyder?

"I must say you don't make things easy for a man," he told Brianne after they were seated in his office. "I had a talk with the detective in charge of your case and another conversation with the District Attorney's office."

She shifted uneasily in her chair. "You're not sounding very positive."

"Probably because they're the ones who feel pretty positive." He pulled a manila folder out of a stack to one side and opened it. "Why didn't you tell me the gun was registered to you?"

Brianne's shock was so great, she was surprised she didn't fall off her chair.

Your brother bought you the gun more than five years ago for protection when there were a lot of robberies in the area. You forgot you even had it.

"Trey gave it to me years ago," she explained. "There were a lot of robberies in the area and he was worried about me. I didn't even remember I owned a gun." The moment she said the latter, she knew she was in trouble. Especially when Rhyder looked skeptical and even Pete didn't look all that pleased with her answer.

"Well, you must have remembered it that night in order to get it out," Rhyder muttered. "What I would like to do is recreate the events of that evening. I want to start with Michael first showing up at your house."

Her mind was a complete blank.

Mathias? She called out mentally. *Mathias, where the hell are you?*

Silence.

She could feel her smile quivering.

"I don't remember that night," she said honestly. *Mathias, I am calling you. Beeping you. Screaming for you! Answer me! Now!*

Rhyder took a breath. "Then we'll just have to start at a point you do remember and go from there."

Brianne's throat muscles worked convulsively. "I remember hearing Trey's voice. He sounded shocked. I looked down and saw Michael lying on the floor. I was holding a gun. Then I fainted."

"What about when Michael arrived at the house?" Pete inquired. "What was his attitude then?"

Mathias, if you know what's good for you, you will help me out now! she screamed inside her head.

Still nothing.

Her smile wobbled dangerously. "I don't remember."

Rhyder muttered something under his breath. "Brianne, you have to remember something. This won't work in court, believe me. They're going to want answers, and they're not going to believe you don't remember anything about that night." He looked impatient. "Think back to your getting ready for your date. What time did Michael arrive?"

She closed her eyes, once again willing Mathias to give her some answers.

If you weren't already dead, I'd kill you! she mentally screamed.

Rhyder tapped his pen against the fingers of his opposite hand. "Okay, another approach. Stand up," he ordered, rising to his feet.

She didn't think twice as she obeyed.

"Let's try a walk through. What was the first thing you said when Michael showed up?" he asked. His patience was rapidly slipping. Rhyder was known as an excellent lawyer, but he didn't suffer fools lightly.

Brianne could feel the shakes start at her ankles and work their way up. "I really don't know," she whispered, feeling pain work its way up her body, too.

Pete couldn't stop staring at her. "Bri, you have to remember *something* from that night," he persisted.

She hated crying. She really did. She always believed it did nothing for her. Her eyes would swell up and turn red. Her mascara ran and her face turned puffy. No, crying was not attractive on her at all. She didn't want to think the real Brianne could cry prettily and she wasn't about to find out. Not when she knew she would be bawling like a baby once she started.

"I am not lying. I honestly don't remember anything from that night," she argued, still fighting tears.

The men stood side by side, looking at her as if asking her to pull the other leg.

"You don't understand," she cried out. "I can't remember because..." She took several deep breaths.

"Because why?" Rhyder brusquely demanded when she didn't continue.

Pete looked as if he wasn't sure what was going to happen, but his expression indicated he was feeling that anything he was about to hear wouldn't be good.

Brianne begged, pleaded and screamed for Mathias to give her answers, but it was as if he had never been there.

You'd think he'd have an answering machine or something, she thought as she faced the two grim-faced men. What was she going to tell them?

That answer hit her like a streak of blinding light. Not as word from Mathias, but from deep within herself. There was only one answer she could give. And she didn't think they were going to appreciate it.

"I can't tell you anything because I don't know anything," she said honestly.

"Bri, you have to know something," Pete said slowly. "If we go over that night step by step, you just might be able to recall how it happened."

She wasn't going to cry. She vowed it. She turned to him. "Pete, I can't tell you anything about that night for one very good reason," she said quietly, hating herself for the tears filling her eyes.

"What good reason?" Rhyder asked.

She took another deep breath. She already knew it wasn't going to be easy.

"What reason, Brianne?" Rhyder asked again. It was clear his limited patience was long gone.

"The reason being I wasn't there," she said swiftly, before she lost her nerve.

While Rhyder turned away, Pete stared at her, willing the truth. "You were found standing over the body with the gun in your hand, so how can you say you weren't there?"

"It's very easy to say, but hard to comprehend. Because while Brianne Sinclair was there, *I* wasn't," she explained.

"That makes no sense at all!" Pete exploded.

She glared at him. "It makes a hell of a lot of sense when I'm not Brianne Sinclair."

Rhyder uttered a few choice words. Pete looked as if he had just been poleaxed.

Brianne was even more determined not to break down in front of them. "I knew you wouldn't believe me." She picked up her purse. "But it's the truth. When I found myself thrust inside Brianne Sinclair's body, Michael was already dead."

"No wonder her family's attorney recommended an insanity defense," Rhyder muttered.

Brianne shook her head. "Never mind. You're right. They're right. No one will ever believe me because the story is too crazy." She stared at Pete, silently imploring him to believe her, but there was too much doubt written on his face. "I could prove it," she said softly. Then she ran out of the office.

As the door closed after her retreating figure, Rhyder turned to Pete.

"You've taken on some strange cases in the past, but this one takes the cake, old buddy."

Pete felt his inner turmoil doing a number on his stomach. There had been something in Brianne's eyes as she pleaded with him to believe her... Who said it wasn't true? Stranger things had happened. He grabbed his jacket and shrugged it on. "I'm going to find out what's going on."

"Good idea. When you find out, let me know."

Pete stopped before he left the room. "What if she is telling the truth, Rhyder? What if the real Brianne is off somewhere else and this other woman is completely innocent?"

"And what if Brianne Sinclair really killed her fiancé and she's hoping this scheme of hers will work? If nothing else, it could guarantee her a long stay at a quiet clinic somewhere."

Pete thought of the night before. His gut feelings had never failed him before, and this time he was positive he hadn't made love with a murderess.

He shook his head. "No, for some completely weird reason, I think she just might be telling the truth. I intend to go after her and find out what she does know."

Rhyder shook his head. "You're not thinking with your brain."

"Yes, I am." Pete let himself out and hurried to the elevator. He only hoped he could catch up with her in the parking lot. He fumed the entire time he waited for the elevator and whistled impatiently as it descended to the lobby. When he finally ran outside, he caught a glimpse of blond hair a short distance away.

"Brianne!" he shouted, running after her. "Wait up!"

She looked over her shoulder, saw him and picked up her pace. She had barely reached her car when he caught up, grasping her arm and swinging her around to face him. His heart sank when he noticed the tears trailing down her cheeks.

"Let me go!" She pulled away. "You're such a bastard, Pete Hackett! You've always been one!"

He would have grabbed her again but didn't want anyone to think he was attacking her. The way she spoke, as if she had known him for years, nagged at him.

"We need to talk."

"Why? So you can again tell me I'm lying?" she said bitterly. "Well, I'm not lying. And I can prove it."

"Then let's go somewhere and talk about it." He gestured to his car.

"I'd rather drive myself."

"Fine. Meet me at my apartment." Pete walked away, silently praying she wouldn't take off before they had a chance to talk. As he pulled out in traffic, he heaved a sigh of relief when he saw the red BMW behind him.

He drove on automatic pilot as he ran through events since he'd first met Brianne. From the beginning, she had not been able to give him all the answers he wanted. Was that why? Because she might look and talk like Brianne Sinclair, but her memories, her emotions, maybe her soul, belonged to someone else?

It defied all logic, the left side of his brain stated. How could she claim she wasn't who she is?

Pete wasn't sure, but he was determined to be open-minded enough to listen. He only hoped he was doing the right thing.

He stood outside his car as Brianne parked hers, and waited until she approached him. They walked silently upstairs to his apartment. When they stepped inside, Pete was hit with memories of the last time they had been in here. Then, emotions had boiled over. They barely had made it to the bedroom.

Now it was as if they were strangers.

"Wine?" he asked in a quiet voice, feeling the pain deep within himself.

She shook her head. "It's not exactly my favorite beverage," she murmured.

Pete thought about an interesting tidbit he'd picked up from Lisa Winters—Brianne only drank wine or champagne, since she claimed any other form of alcohol gave her a headache.

"I have some tequila." He walked into the kitchen and opened the cabinet that held his meager supply of liquor. Tequila wasn't one of his favorite drinks, but something told him he was going to be in for a few surprises.

When he returned to the living room, he found the drapes pulled open and Brianne standing at the window. He was struck dumb by the purity of her profile as she stood there staring out, but something about her stance said she wasn't looking at anything in particular, rather, pictures pulled from her memory banks. He waited until she felt his presence and turned to face him. She walked over to the couch and sat down, accepting the glass he held out. She downed the tequila without a grimace.

Pete gulped down his own drink, waiting for the explosion of heat in the pit of his stomach. He leaned forward in the chair with his elbows resting on his knees. He rolled the glass between his palms.

"How do you know you're not Brianne Sinclair?" he asked quietly.

Something in the tone of his voice told her he was willing to listen. She only hoped he would believe her and not think she was making up some ridiculous story.

She licked her lips. "I remember dying."

What felt like an icy blanket settled over Pete. "How did you die?" He found it difficult to force the words between his lips.

This was what she feared the most. Could she make him believe her? Maybe she would have been better off lying to Rhyder. She knew how to make a man believe anything she said. Why hadn't she done that instead of starting this?

"I was stabbed." Her reply was spoken so low he almost didn't hear the words.

"Stabbed by whom?"

"My boyfriend killed me." She lifted her head, willing him to look at her. "I discovered he was dealing drugs and lost my temper. When I threatened to call the police, he shoved me around and I shoved back. Before I knew it, he had his knife out and stabbed me." She stopped.

Pete felt a chill invade his body.

"That doesn't explain how you ended up as Brianne," he said slowly.

She knew she was fighting an uphill battle, but she couldn't stop now. "I was angry when he stabbed me. At first I felt numb, then I felt the pain. Then I felt nothing. It was as if I was floating above my body. I was angry because I knew no one would know he'd killed me. After that, it was dark. I remember screaming how it all wasn't fair. The next thing I knew it was light around me and I was standing over Michael's body. There was a mirror nearby and when I looked in it, I could see I was no longer myself. But for a moment, I thought I could see my real self, too. It didn't last long."

For a second, a wild thought invaded Pete's mind. A thought he instantly dismissed because he refused to believe such a thing was possible.

"Who are you really?"

She looked away for a moment. Her lips moved, but he couldn't hear the words.

"Who are you?" he asked again. She closed her eyes. "Allie Walker."

Denial bounced around in his head. He sat frozen in the chair.

"No."

She nodded. "That's why I chose you to help me."

Pete jumped to his feet and paced the length of the room. "This is all bull!" he exploded. "You're only saying that because you know I want to find Allie's killer. You learned all you needed to know about her death from newspaper stories."

"Reading newspapers didn't tell me your middle name is Aloysius. Or that you were named after your uncle."

He shook his head violently, refusing to believe what he was hearing. "You have an unlimited bank account, honey. You could have learned that in many ways."

Brianne took a deep breath. "We met more than eight years ago. You patrolled the area where the coffee shop was and you stopped for lunch. You told me my legs should be considered illegal because my skirt was short, but you wouldn't cite me as long as I continued serving up the coffee."

Pete winced at the memory. "My ex-partner could have told you that," he said harshly. Snippets of time spent with Brianne came back to him. Inconsistencies tried to explain themselves even as he dismissed them.

"John was killed by a gang member during a shootout four years ago," she whispered, still watching him with eyes that reflected pain, sorrow and a lot of regrets.

Pete could feel the pressure building up behind his sternum. "It's too crazy."

"Is it? You once asked me if I could be anyone in the world, who would I want to be? I pointed to Brianne Sinclair's picture in the paper and said I wanted to be her," she said quietly. "I wanted to be rich and go to parties and travel. I said then I wouldn't have any worries. Instead, I ended up accused of murdering her fiancé." Her lips twisted. "Since I somehow ended up in her body, I've had nothing but problems."

He waved his hands. "No, I can't believe this."

Brianne stood up. "Do you think I made up this ridiculous story for the hell of it?" she asked. "I had no idea what had happened. I was thrown in a jail cell, and for all I knew, was going to be there for a long time. If it hadn't been for Mathias explaining things to me about Brianne, I would have been a basket case."

Pete shot her a sharp look. "Who's Mathias?"

She grimaced. And she thought it was difficult to explain her ending up in another body! "I don't know."

"Someone explains things to you and you don't know?" He uttered a harsh laugh. "Try again!"

"He's a voice in my head!" she shouted. "That's all I can tell you. When I was in jail, I kept asking what was going on, and a voice suddenly sounded inside my head and told me I wanted to be Brianne and voilà, I was her."

"What happened to the real Brianne?" He still refused to believe what he was hearing.

She shook her head. "Mathias said her heart couldn't handle the shock. He didn't explain it all to me, so I guess he meant the shock of Michael's death."

"Then why hasn't he told you what happened that night?"

"I don't know. He said it was up to me to make things right. He just never said what that would be," she said sadly.

He suddenly wished for a cigarette. What he wouldn't give for one!

"I'm sorry, but this is too fantastic," he said finally.

Brianne looked down at her hands. "Then I guess there's only one thing I can say to make you believe me," she murmured. "There's something about you only you, one other person and I know."

"Oh really?" he drawled.

She nodded. "That's because that other person told me about it the day the two of you broke up. And I know for a fact she didn't tell anyone else. She moved out of the state not long after that."

"Oh really?" he said again sarcastically. "And what could this fascinating piece of information be that only I and another person and Allie know? My shoe size? My mother's maiden name? What?"

Brianne lifted her head and waited until he looked directly at her. She knew what she was about to say would, without a doubt, convince him she was who she claimed to be. Not only would he be convinced, but it was going to send him into a fury. It was something she had kept to herself all this time. Not even the threat of death would have persuaded her to part with this piece of news. Ironic that it was her death that was persuading her to part with it. Now she had to make him believe the truth. And then all she had to do was pray he wouldn't hate her for knowing about it all this time.

She took a deep breath before dropping her verbal bomb and winced as she waited for the awaited explosion.

''The first time you and Jennifer Carlson went to bed, you couldn't get it up.''

Chapter Thirteen

"I have to be honest. And I'm not one to gossip about someone who isn't here to defend herself, but I never liked Jennifer." Brianne, oblivious to the shock etched on Pete's face, chattered on. "I mean, the woman always felt she was better than everyone else. Not to mention she constantly wore blue eye shadow. That color did absolutely nothing for her. I told her that once and she said I was only saying it because I was jealous. Jealous! Ha! Of someone who wore colored contact lenses when she didn't need glasses, only because they made her eyes look bluer? Someone who'd had a tummy tuck, butt tuck and implants?" she confided. "Then she decided that wasn't enough and had liposuction done on her thighs. She was too lazy to exercise but willing to go through hell to keep her body firm."

Still staring at Brianne as if she was a specter from another dimension, Pete backed up until the back of his knees hit the edge of the chair. He collapsed into the seat and could only sit there. His face alternately turned white and purple as he watched her. His mouth hung open as he listened to her rapid-fire speech. This time he listened to her as a detective, not as a man. He picked out distinctive speech patterns, word choices, and it all fell into place. The longer he looked at her, the more resemblance he saw to a brash brunette he used to see on a daily basis. A woman whose murder he was also investigating!

No wonder stories he heard via Brianne's friends and work colleagues didn't jell with what he saw when he was with her. They were talking about the woman they'd known before Michael Matthews was murdered. Pete had met her after the fact and by then, she was no longer the same person!

"Oh my God," he whispered hoarsely, feeling his world turn completely upside down. His stomach sank as if he'd just dropped off a tall roller-coaster track. "You really are Allie."

She turned to him. 'I told you I was and I never lie. Pete, you look as if you've seen a ghost." She suddenly laughed. "Hmm, I guess in a sense you have, haven't you? Admittedly, I've had more time to get used to this than you have. When I first looked in the mirror and saw her face instead of mine, I was ready to freak out. Considering the circumstances at the time, I wish I had," she said dryly, waving her hand back and forth in an airy circle. "This is not how I planned my life, believe me."

Pete groaned and buried his face in his hands. "No, this all has to be some incredible dream." His words were muffled. "None of this is real."

Brianne took pity on him. She edged off the couch and walked over to the chair, crouching down and placing her hands on his knees. She drew them back when he flinched from her touch. She schooled her features to hide her pain at his rejection, which was written even more explicitly on his face when he looked up.

"Why did you come to me?" he demanded.

"I told you at the time. I wanted the best, and no matter what, you are the best. I knew you could find out the truth for me."

Pete's laughter was as harsh and raw as his features. "Great. You wanted to be rich and have your picture in the papers. You got that in spades." He pushed himself out of the chair, almost unbalancing her in the process. He began walking back and forth in an attempt to work out the confused feelings in his body. He didn't look at her the entire time. "You know, I always admired you. You always seemed to have it together. Okay, you had lousy taste in men, but no one's perfect." If he was babbling, he was unaware of it. "Still, you always went on. And now I find out you've been playing games with me. What'd you decide to do? Hire me just to give an old friend a financial leg up?" He spun around. "And what was last night?"

Brianne's eyes were shadowed with the same pain. "Last night was more than I could ever hope for. It was like a dream come true," she whispered. "Maybe I shouldn't have told you so soon—about me being Allie—but I had to. I know telling you has changed things."

"It sure as hell has!"

It doesn't sound as if you're having good luck with him.

She mentally ordered her guardian voice to get lost.

"You've now got everything you ever wanted. Including Rhyder, who will get you off the murder charge," he said harshly. "You don't need me anymore."

Brianne blinked back the tears burning her eyes. "Oh yes, I have everything I ever wanted. I only had to be killed to achieve it," she said quietly.

Pete's hands clenched into tight fists. "This is rich. There's finally solid proof that Whit killed you, except you're not you anymore." He stopped in midpace. He kept shaking his head as he tried to take it all in. "Now I understand why you don't know anything about Michael's murder. You aren't lying and you don't actually have shock-induced amnesia. You don't know because you weren't even there!"

Brianne could feel the pain tighten in a coil deep within her body. She placed one hand on the floor to keep her balance as she straightened up.

"I shouldn't have told you," she whispered, picking her purse up from the couch. "It's just that you kept asking me questions I couldn't answer, and I knew if I kept evading them you'd think I was lying. I wanted to tell you so badly, but Mathias told me it wouldn't be a good idea."

"And Mathias is—?" He rocked one hand in a wigwag motion to invite her explanation.

"To be honest, I have no idea what he is. I have to assume by his name he is a he, but it took me awhile to get even that out of him." She opened her purse to pull out her car keys. "Look, I'm sorry I got you involved in all this. I'll call Rhyder and tell him I'm going to agree to my family's suggestion about the temporary-insanity plea. Just send me a bill for whatever I might owe you." Her head was bowed as she walked to the door. Before she could turn the knob, her arm was grasped none too gently and she was spun around so quickly her purse dropped to the floor, spilling its contents. Pete's body effectively pinned her against the door. The expression on his face was fierce as he leaned in with one arm either side of her body.

"Tell me one thing," he said roughly, keeping her trapped against the unforgiving wood by his equally unforgiving body. "What about us?"

Her throat worked convulsively as she fought to keep her tears contained. Her chin wobbled as she stared at him. She couldn't help it. She raised one hand and laid her palm against his cheek. His skin was rough from his late-day beard, but it didn't matter to her. Her thumb rubbed lightly over his lower lip, which parted slightly at her touch.

"I already told you," she said in a voice that was barely audible. "You mean the world to me. I have never experienced such beauty, such joy, until you. I don't want it to end, Pete. Please don't hate me. I don't want to lose you."

He muttered what could have been a curse or a prayer as he dropped his head and captured her lips in a fiery kiss that threatened to consume the two of them. The inferno that had ensnared them the night before flared up instantly as they clung to each other with a desperation born from the inconceivable situation that had brought them together.

Brianne's tears flowed freely along with the relief she felt at telling Pete. The wetness dampened Pete's face and lips as he pressed hard kisses along her face. His kisses weren't meant to reassure her. He wanted to let her know he was willing to accept what had happened to her that incredible night. For the moment, this was the only way he could do it.

"Don't cry, honey," he begged in between kisses. "We can make it right. I know we can. I'll find a way. Please don't cry."

She knew he was telling her that to make her feel better, just as she'd tried to reassure him earlier. But she was starting to fear the worst.

"How?" she sniffed, burying her face against his shoulder. "I know how a murder was committed, but since I was the victim, I can't testify. I'm accused of another murder, except I know I didn't commit it, but can't prove it since I was holding the gun at the time. None of it came out right. My dream turned into a nightmare."

Pete could feel her tears seep through the cotton of his shirt and warm his skin. He held on to her as if he was afraid he could lose her at any second.

Disjointed thoughts raced through his head. Memories of early morning coffee spent with Allie when she started work. How many times had she coaxed him out of a bad mood or a morose one because a bust went wrong? When he'd started his own business, she'd done even more bullying to keep him going. He realized that he'd gone into Charlie's, not for the food, but for Allie! No wonder he'd felt such a strong attraction for Brianne from the moment he met her. It was because she was Allie. He hadn't lost her, after all!

His arms tightened around her. The realization of what all of this really meant hit him like a ton of bricks. He wasn't sure how it had happened, but somehow they were being given a second chance. He told himself that if he had any brains in his head he wouldn't blow it this time.

"No, it didn't, Brianne," he said finally, deliberately using her new name to let her know he more than understood. "You're wrong. For some reason this was all meant to be—your ending up in Brianne Sinclair's body, your fiancé's murder and your seeking me out. We're supposed to have this."

A faint glimmer of hope shone in her eyes. "You think so?" Her shoulders rose and fell as she sighed. "I was afraid that I was only going to be in her body until I somehow solved the murder, then I'd end up in somebody else's."

Pete blinked, more than a little confused by her logic. And a tad worried that she could be right. Could he lose her now that he'd realized how badly he needed her?

"But Mathias said this was reality, not television," she continued.

He couldn't help it. He wasn't sure if it was the insanity of the past hour or lack of sleep or what, he just knew that he had to laugh. He rested his forehead against hers and chuckled.

"Sounds as if this Mathias is a character," he commented between chuckles.

"No kidding. Talk about a voice with an attitude," she muttered, still hanging on to him.

She still couldn't shake her fear that he was suddenly going to decide she was from out of this world, literally, and take off for parts unknown. Considering what she had just told him, she wouldn't blame him a bit.

Except holding on to him, feeling the warmth of his body through his clothing, inhaling the warm, musky scent of his skin, brought back a few other memories. She was suddenly determined not to let him go. When his hips bumped against hers, she felt evidence that something else hadn't changed.

"Pete?" she asked in a small voice.

"Hmm?" He was too caught up in the feel of her against him to think about anything else—except how close, and yet so far away, the bedroom was.

"We're not going to stand here all night, are we?"

"I wasn't sure if you'd decide to leave."

"Only if you want me to."

It didn't take him long to think about it. "You really want to head back to that mansion of horrors housing the wicked witch of South Pasadena?"

She looked up at him coyly. "No."

Pete pretended to think about it. "Want to go out and get something to eat?"

Brianne smiled as she toyed with the buttons on his shirt. "Not really." The first button parted company with the buttonhole. Then the second one did, and her fingers found their way beneath the soft fabric to his bare chest. She idly ran her nails around a copper-colored nipple, which rose at her touch.

"Hell." He bent down, gathered her up in his arms and walked toward the bedroom. "That Chinese place down the street delivers. I'll just press five."

BRIANNE'S DRESS now decorated the top of Pete's chest of drawers, with his shirt draped over it. His jeans and her bra hung haphazardly over the lamp, and her stockings and garter belt were flung in three different directions, with his socks and underwear scattered nearby. The bed looked like another war zone with the pillows pushed to the floor and blankets and sheets hanging off the side. The couple lying in the middle of the bed didn't seem to care.

If the air was cool, Brianne didn't notice, what with Pete's body half covering hers. If her body felt as if it had been shot into another dimension, she didn't care. Not when he had been there with her all the way. Now she was content to rest with eyes closed and relish the replete feeling in her body. She would have been content to just lie there even though Pete's hand, stroking her side from just under her arm down to her hip, was setting off a few tiny explosions.

"You are incredible," she said drowsily. "Are you sure you aren't taking any special vitamins or doing some series of weird oriental exercises?"

"Nope." His breath was warm against her cheek, since his head was resting next to hers on the pillow. "Don't need anything where you're concerned." His stroking hand grew slower and slower. "Although I have a pretty good idea I won't be able to move for at least the next ten days."

Brianne smiled. "Oh, I think I can inspire you to move before then." Her smile grew broader as another thought occurred to her.

Pete watched her with a great deal of caution. He was rapidly learning that her smiles usually meant another shock was in store for him. "What are you thinking about now?"

Still smiling as if she was the cat with the canary in her mouth, she lifted her head an inch so she could better see his face. "Amazing, isn't it? You never have that problem with me that you had with Jennifer. Which means it must have been something about her that..." she paused as she searched for the correct word "...didn't *inspire* you."

His body shook with laughter. "You are bad. Very bad."

"Mmm, and you love it," she purred.

Pete moved enough to pull a blanket over them. He shifted so that Brianne's head rested in the curve of his shoulder. She turned her head and pressed a kiss against his collarbone, tasting the salt of his skin.

The late-afternoon light was rapidly diminishing, leaving them in a pale twilight. For the moment, they were content with their shared silence. Except she couldn't get the events of the past few hours out of her mind. From the absolute high her meeting with the clothing managers had inspired, to the distress in Rhyder's office...to the emotional low as she confessed all to Pete and to the fireworks of only a few moments ago, she felt as if she had been riding on a runaway roller coaster. She feared the ride wasn't about to end.

"What are we going to tell Rhyder?" she asked quietly.

Pete didn't answer right away. "Something tells me he isn't going to believe the truth."

"You didn't want to believe me and I had concrete evidence of my identity to give you." She snuggled closer to his side. She didn't want to leave here, but didn't know how to convey those thoughts to him.

"I guess I better start hunting harder to find Michael's killer then," Pete mused. "Which means I want to talk to your brother, sister-in-law and mother.''

''Better you than me,'' she said wryly.

He brushed her bangs from her forehead and touched his lips to the smooth skin. ''See if your Mathias will help us out with some pointed questions.''

''He said it was up to me to find out.''

''It wouldn't hurt to ask.''

''With Mathias, a simple request turns into a major chore.'' Brianne mentally took stock of herself. ''You did say that Chinese place down the street delivered?''

He chuckled. ''Yeah. I even have their number programmed into my speed dialer. Along with a pizza place, Mexican food and a small bakery.''

Brianne sat up. ''Then why don't you call down there and see if they'll rustle up some sweet-and-sour or maybe *kung pao* chicken, barbecued pork, fried rice and chicken chow mein.'' She closed her eyes in thought. ''Do they have broccoli beef? I love that. And shrimp.''

''Don't forget the fortune cookies,'' Pete muttered, stunned by the amount of food she was requesting.

She shook her head. ''No, I'm watching my weight. *Pete!*'' she squealed when he started tickling her.

Within twenty minutes their food was delivered. Pete pulled on his jeans to accept the delivery, then carried the containers into the bedroom.

''All right, we'll call this a business dinner,'' he told her. ''We'll figure out what to tell Rhyder, how we'll handle your family, and once we've finished eating, we'll discuss something a little more personal.'' He eyed the way one of his T-shirts draped her body, feeling a renewal of that old hunger. And here he thought that had been assuaged for a while. Now he knew his thirst for her would never be satisfied. And another emotion was taking root inside him—one he hadn't ever thought would come over him. But then, he hadn't reckoned on a sassy wench named Brianne coming into his life, either.

Her fingers dripping with the thick sweet-and-sour sauce, Brianne held a piece of chicken against his lips. "If we're talking business, I have something else I'd like to discuss," she said, after he'd taken the offering in his teeth.

Pete should have known she'd deliberately wait until his mouth was full so that he couldn't readily argue with her.

She picked up one of the napkins and delicately dabbed at his lips. "I want to trap Whit," she said huskily, forking up some rice and holding it to his mouth.

He started to speak, but couldn't. He quickly chewed and swallowed. "Where did that come from?"

"I thought about it while you paid the delivery man," she explained. "Actually, I've been thinking about it off and on for days, but it's been occurring to me more and more lately. You've had no luck in finding proof he killed me, right?"

He nodded, wary of the way her mind was working. Now he understood why Brianne was so pushy at times. She was just acting the way Allie always did.

After feeding Pete another forkful of rice, she took some for herself.

"All I know is what the newspaper said, and that was supposedly that someone broke into the apartment, Whit and I surprised him and the robber killed me and beat him up.''

"That's the story he gave, and with no witnesses, it stuck more than I liked," he said darkly. "I went to all the bars he hung out at. There's a lot of people willing to come forward and swear they heard him kill you, but he also has a few friends willing to swear the opposite. Rick has had to leave the case pretty much closed, since nothing could be found."

She appeared lost in thought for several minutes as she took bites from each container.

"When I came home that night, I was dead tired after working two shifts," she said. "I figured Whit would still be at work and I'd planned on a hot bath. When I got to the apartment, I found the door open and Whit inside talking on the phone." She grimaced. "He was setting up a drug deal. He'd sworn to me he'd stopped dealing, but he was making arrangements to meet someone. I heard him and I just lost it. I went in there swinging and yelling. He hit me a couple times, I hit back and next thing I knew..." She stopped. She discovered the memories were still strong within her, turning into pictures in her mind. She started trembling violently and had no sense of Pete's arms warmly surrounding her. "He had a knife. I didn't feel anything at first. Then I felt cold." She knew she was babbling and hated herself for it, but couldn't seem to stop. "Then warm. Then it was as if I was on the outside looking in. I could see myself falling to the floor, blood flowing down my chest and Whit standing over me. He realized what he'd done and he didn't care. Then things got black and I was so angry because I knew he would get away with it and I didn't think it was fair. Oh, Pete!'' she sobbed, her fingernails digging into his arm, which curved around her front. "I shouldn't have to remember all of this!''

"Maybe you're supposed to.'' He felt as sick as she did as he heard what had happened that night. And he cursed life for not giving him a way to nail Whit.

Brianne took several deep breaths to calm her racing emotions. "You're right, maybe by my remembering that night I can do something about it.'' She suddenly leaned over and picked up Pete's phone.

"What are you doing?''

"Why, honey, I'm going to call a creep and hopefully scare the hell out of him,'' she informed him in an exact duplication of Allie's voice. She quickly punched in a series of numbers.

For the life of him, Pete couldn't think of a single argument against her plan. Especially since he didn't know what she was going to do.

Brianne waited. "Better yet,'' she whispered. "He has the answering machine on.'' She waited another minute, took a deep breath and spoke in a husky whisper, "Whit, sweet cheeks, you know who this is? That's right, lover. You only thought you killed me. But I wasn't going to leave you that easily. Keep an eye out for me, Whit. I'll be coming to see you.'' She hung up quickly, then burst out laughing. "Can you imagine how he's going to feel when he hears that message?''

"Probably the same way I do right now,'' Pete muttered, uneasy over what he'd just heard.

"If nothing else, he's going to start looking over his shoulder. I'll give him another call in a day or so. Just so he won't think it's someone's idea of a sick joke.''

"What do you hope to accomplish with that crazy stunt?" he demanded. He wasn't about to admit he still felt chills traveling up his spine at hearing Allie's voice come out of Brianne's mouth.

"Maybe it will scare him enough to slip up," she replied. As if the call had been a catharsis for past pain, she stabbed her fork into one of the containers, brought out a piece of broccoli beef and ate it. "You know, this is really good. I haven't had good Chinese food in so long."

"Princess, I have to admit you've got style," Pete said with great admiration as he took the fork out of her hand, speared a treat out of another container and placed it against her lips.

"Now that I've got Brianne out of that boring wardrobe, I do," she quipped.

Chapter Fourteen

"You son of a bitch!"

The snarl was Pete's first warning. The fist thrown in his direction was his second. Whit threw himself at Pete with the ferocity of a crazed man.

"What the hell is your problem?" Pete panted as he ducked another incoming punch. The first one that connected with his jaw hurt like hell, and he wasn't about to allow himself to get beaten up until he'd heard a good reason why. And then he'd make sure to beat the hell out of the guy.

Whit bore down on him with fury in his eyes. "You were the one who made that call last night," he accused. "And it wasn't funny. You are a sick man, Hackett."

Well, well, well. Pete kept his expression noncommittal. "I don't know what your problem is, but I didn't call you last night. There's no reason in this world I'd want to call you."

Whit wiped the back of his hand across his mouth. "You've been askin' around about me and Allie. You still think I killed her, and since no one could tell you anything that proves me guilty, you decided to start with these creepy phone calls to make me say stuff that isn't true. You tell that bitch you had call me that she's in just as much trouble as you are.''

Pete stepped back and studied Whit's face. There was no mistaking the anger written on his features, but he read something else there. Whit's eyes looked wild as if he'd sniffed something recently, and Pete was positive he wasn't out sniffing flowers. What he saw on Whit's face was pure fear. The man's skin was paler than usual and damp with sweat—the kind of sweat that means a person is deathly afraid of something he can't see. Whit knew he was guilty of killing Allie. He'd stood there and watched her die. The SOB had thought he was free and clear, until he'd heard a voice on his answering machine last night. A voice he considered to have come from the grave.

Pete held his hands out in front of him to show Whit he wasn't carrying any kind of weapon. ''Look, man, I don't know what you've been ingesting lately, but I'd say you got hold of some bad stuff. I'd really take it up with your supplier. I didn't call you last night. I'd have no reason to. And sure, I've been asking around about you. What'd you expect me to do? Allie was a good friend, and to be honest, I think you're scum. All my investigation got me was squat. So maybe your story is true. Just remember I didn't find anything.''

''Yeah, you wanted her,'' Whit sneered. ''You were hot for her and you were jealous because I had her. Well, you're not pinning anything on me.'' He backed away. ''You stay out of my business, Hackett. Next time you might not be so lucky.''

Pete didn't move an inch. ''Hey, Whit. What if it was Allie who phoned you?'' he asked.

Whit's eyes practically bugged out. "She's dead!" he screamed. "Dammit, she's dead!" He turned and ran off.

Pete waited until Whit was out of sight before heaving a sigh of relief. "Damn her," he chuckled, ironically using the curse as a form of affection. "I gotta give it to her. She freaked him out good."

He continued on down the street toward Rhyder's office. He was still trying to figure out what he was going to say to his friend without it sounding as if it came from the *Twilight Zone*.

"Gee, Rhyder, you're not going to believe this," he said under his breath, as he waited for the elevator. "But Brianne isn't who you think she is."

"Oh really? Then who is she?"

Pete spun around. "Dammit, can't you give a guy some warning?" he grumbled. He had always prided himself on his sharp ears. The only man who seemed to have the knack of slipping up behind him was Rhyder.

The lawyer merely looked amused. "Not my fault your hearing is failing. That's one of the first things to go, isn't it?"

Pete's retort was earthy and to the point.

"So what do you think I'm not going to believe?" Rhyder asked as they entered the elevator.

He looked around. "Let's wait until we get inside your office."

Rhyder was quiet on the trip upstairs and down the hall to his office. He stopped by Sofia's desk for messages and gestured for Pete to enter.

"Now, what is it?"

"First off, I didn't want to believe this, but I swear to God, it's all true," Pete prefaced.

"Fine. It's all true. *What* is all true?" He was rapidly losing his patience. Pete took a deep breath and prayed Rhyder wouldn't decide to have him committed after he finished his story. He began with his first meeting with Brianne, the comments he'd heard from her friends and colleagues that didn't agree with what he'd observed about her. He went on to other little details, such as Brianne drinking tequila shooters with him, and Allie only drinking that, when Brianne was known for drinking wine and champagne only. He decided to delete conveniently the night they'd spent together and went on to Brianne's confession the night before. Even to her ability to imitate Allie's voice and her phone call to Whit's answering machine. By the time he ended his narration with his run-in with Whit, he felt as if he'd run a marathon.

Rhyder sat behind his desk, his hands laced together on the blotter. Nothing on his face gave away what he was thinking. "You do realize if anyone else had told me this story I would have immediately ushered them out of my office."

"No matter how crazy it sounds, it's all true, Rhyder. I swear it." Pete shook his head as if trying clear it. "She told me enough last night to convince me she's Allie."

"So who did you make love to last night? Brianne or Allie?"

Pete's eyes narrowed. "By rights, I should take a swing at you for that."

"You won't because you're feeling like hell as it is." Rhyder pulled out a file folder from the small pile on the side of his desk and opened it. "If I took this story to the D.A., I'd be laughed out of his office. Her court date is coming up fast and I'm going to need everything I can get to help her. I'll tell you now—what you've just told me won't help her one bit. You know that, don't you?"

Pete nodded. "I have some ideas and I'm planning to do some more digging. I have an appointment with her brother tomorrow morning and her mother in the afternoon."

Rhyder lifted an eyebrow as he settled back in his chair. "I'm impressed. I thought her mother considered you the lowest of the low. How did you manage to convince her to talk to you?"

He squirmed in his seat. "I let her think that if she could convince me Brianne's best interest lay in the diminished-capacity plea, I would persuade her daughter to take that course."

"You do realize that if she thinks you're now on her mother's side she'll hate your guts," Rhyder drawled.

Pete absently patted his pockets, searching for the pack of cigarettes that was no longer there. It didn't matter that he'd quit long ago. When he felt stressed out, he always looked for those cigarettes. And vowed he wouldn't get caught up in the habit again. "She won't find out."

"You don't think her mother won't tell her? How much you wanna bet the minute you're out the door that she's on the horn to Brianne?"

"She'll keep quiet because she wants my help in persuading her daughter. She's got it in her head I have some kind of Svengali influence over her. I'm willing to let her think that if it means she'll talk to me."

Rhyder chuckled. "I wonder where she got that idea?" He held his hands up in silent surrender when Pete scowled at him. "Okay, okay. Just tell me one thing. What do you hope to find out from her?"

Pete was silent for a moment, rubbing his chin in thought. "If I'm lucky, I'll find out the truth."

BRIANNE HAD NEVER FELT as energized as she did that day. Considering she'd had so little sleep the past few nights, she should have felt like a walking zombie. Instead, she fairly danced into her office.

"Everyone has ideas," Gwen announced, following her boss inside. She held up sheets of paper. "It's as if all of a sudden they understand what you want to do and they want to help. Well, except for Mrs. Roscoe and Mrs. Shaw."

Brianne sorted through what appeared to be haphazardly written notes, but the more she read, the more excited she got.

"They're on my side!" she squealed. "They've thought about what I said and they have ideas of their own to add to mine." She spun in a tight circle, then threw her arms up and tapped out a victory dance. When she dropped to her chair, she felt so excited she thought her head might burst with joy. Her entire body vibrated with such energy even Gwen was infected.

"Does this mean we won?" the secretary asked hopefully.

"It means we haven't lost." Brianne took several deep breaths to bring herself back down to earth. "But we have a lot of work ahead of us. Are you prepared to help me kick some more butt around here?"

Her head bobbed up and down. She started back to the doorway, then stopped. Brianne looked up with a question in her eyes.

"Please don't take this the wrong way," Gwen said hesitantly. "But it's as if you're a whole new person now. And you're a lot nicer." Blushing furiously, she almost ran out of the office, quickly closing the door behind her.

Congratulations, Brianne, you've accomplished more than you'll ever know. It was the long-absent Mathias.

She leaned back in her chair. "Is this what Brianne would have wanted?" she asked softly. "It seemed as if she always preferred everything to remain the same. She didn't like to rock the boat, and that's what I've done from the time I came here."

It's what she needed. She needed a purpose in life, but she wasn't allowed to find it. You were able to find that purpose and put all those resources to good use.

For a brief moment a shadow seemed to cross her heart. "Except she isn't here to enjoy it. It doesn't seem right."

She wouldn't have understood any of this, nor would she have required it. You do. It's what you need. You needed an outlet for all that creative energy lying dormant in your brain. Using Brianne's name and power, you were able to make good use of it.

"So you're saying she's happier wherever she is," she murmured.

Brianne was tired of her endless, and fruitless, battles with her mother. She hated the idea of coming into a store where her name was revered, but her suggestions were ignored. She didn't have the drive you have. If anything happened to Trey, the stores would have gone to her, and she didn't want it. You can handle yourself, Brianne, and I am very proud of you.

She laughed softly. ''Thank you, Mathias. I know you had a lot to do with this and I thank you for that, too.''

Actually, you could thank me for Pete, too.

''Why Pete?''

The man loves you, and if I hadn't given you a tiny mental nudge when you needed it, you wouldn't have gone to him. I must say I wasn't happy about that little telephone call you made last night to Whit. Even if you did upset the man so badly he continually looks over his shoulder.

The idea of Pete loving her should have thrilled her instead of leaving her feeling sad. ''He doesn't love me. He loves an image of me, and now he's learned it wasn't me all along. No, I'm sorry, Mathias, for once you're very wrong. As for Whit, if I upset him, good, because he deserves it.''

My dear, I am never wrong. But if you insist on being your stubborn self I guess you'll just have to find out for yourself.

''That's nothing new, is it?'' Brianne roused herself when her phone softly buzzed. It was time to get to work, and she found herself looking forward to the challenge it brought. At the same time, she made a mental note to make another call to Whit. If he was upset over one phone call, what would he feel about two?

WHIT WAS DESPERATE. He'd broken out into a sweat the moment he'd heard Allie's voice on the answering machine last night. In a fit of anger, he'd torn the tape out and stomped on it, in the belief that he was destroying Allie all over again. Yet, he'd had trouble sleeping.

He still believed Hackett was behind the call, even if the bastard swore up and down he wasn't. Whit knew better. He'd wait awhile until he was sure the investigator had his guard down. Then he'd show him who was the better man.

After spending the day wheeling and dealing, he went back to his apartment, running inside when he heard the phone ring. He'd been hoping for a call from his supplier.

"Yeah?"

"Hello, Whit." Allie's brash vowels rang loud and clear across the lines.

He stumbled against the table. "No, it's not you."

"What makes you think so? Because you killed me? Did you honestly think that would stop me?" She laughed softly. "Why did you kill me? Because I found out you were dealing once more? Did you think I wouldn't get angry about your drugs again?" she persisted, ignoring his whimpers. "You promised me you had quit dealing and you hadn't, had you? And I bet you're using, too, aren't you?"

"You bitch! You're dead!" he screamed, and slammed the phone down.

Within seconds it rang again. His fingers trembled as they hovered over the receiver. He didn't want to pick it up, but his mind told him it couldn't be *her* again. No, it was his supplier. It had to be.

"Yeah?" This time he sounded more cautious.

"That was very rude, Whit. I wasn't finished talking to you."

"You're in hell, bitch," he snarled.

"No, Whit, I'm in a much much nicer place than hell. But don't worry, I'm sure you'll find out all about hell when your time comes," she told him. "I'm not going to leave you alone. If you hang up, I'll call again and if you don't talk to me on the phone, I'll just have to come visit you, won't I? Then I can tell your new girlfriend how you break up with a woman." Her voice hardened. "Congratulations, Whit, you're going to find out exactly what it means to be haunted."

Whit didn't settle for hanging up this time. He tore the cord out of the wall outlet and ran out of his apartment. Except as he ran, his fevered brain imagined he could hear the phone still ringing and Allie's voice taunting him.

"I SUPPOSE YOU'RE spending the evening with that private detective again." Olivia's disapproval rang loud and clear over the phone line.

Brianne wasn't going to allow her mother to get to her. "We have a lot of work to do."

"If that's what you choose to call it..." She paused tellingly. "Will you be home in time for breakfast?"

Brianne hated this verbal dancing with her mother. "Actually, I've been thinking about finding a place of my own. I think it's time." *Good going, Brianne, just jump right in with that piece of news,* she scolded herself.

"If I were you, I'd wait to see what happens first. After all, why waste your money on a security deposit

if you're found guilty of murder and sent away?''
With that, Olivia disconnected the call.

Brianne swore under her breath. "No matter what,
she finds a way to really tick me off," she muttered,
jamming papers together with no regard to keeping
them in order. At that moment, all she wanted to do
was get out of her office. That morning, before they
parted, Pete had suggested they meet at his apartment when she left work. He told her he had a few
people he planned on seeing that day.

Thanks to Gwen, Brianne already knew of Pete
talking to the store personnel. It took a lot of will-
power on her part, but she refused to pump the secretary for information. She decided she'd do that to
Pete instead. She knew it would be a lot more fun!

Her spirits were up when she left the store. She carried a shopping bag filled with several impromptu
purchases, which she dropped into the passenger seat.

As it was, she reached Pete's apartment only a few
minutes before he did. He looked harried and out of
sorts.

"Not exactly what I'd call a perfect day," he mumbled, putting his arms around her and kissing her. It
wasn't too long before the light touch deepened. When
he drew back, he was breathing hard. "Tell you what.
Let me grab a shower and we'll continue this after-
wards. Don't forget where we left off." He walked
quickly toward the bedroom, shedding his clothes
along the way.

Brianne was content to stand there and admire the
view of his bare back. Until he slid off his jeans and
briefs. Then she remembered what they had just
started.

"Do you want a beer?" she called out.

"There isn't any," he yelled back.

"There is if someone is nice enough to stop at the store on the way here." She opened the refrigerator door and pulled out a bottle.

On the way to the bathroom, she could hear the shower running. Giving in to temptation, Brianne slipped off her clothing before she entered. The room was steamy from the hot water running behind the frosted-glass door. She smiled at Pete's off-key, but lusty rendition of "Born to be Wild."

"Hey there, wild man." She opened the shower door and stepped inside.

Pete almost fell on the tile as he spun around to face her. He instinctively stepped in front of the spray, so it wouldn't hit her directly. "I am not happy when people try to sneak up on me," he announced, resting his arms on her shoulders. "For you, I'll make an exception."

She reached around him and took the soap out of the holder. "Good, because if you didn't, I'd just have to leave, and you wouldn't want me to do that, would you?" She slowly rubbed the bar between her palms.

Pete's gaze was riveted on her movements. "Funny, you didn't look that dirty to me," he said hoarsely.

Brianne smiled as she set the soap back in the holder. "Oh no, I thought I'd come in here and help you clean up," she murmured, sliding her soapy hands across his chest. When she looked up at him, her eyes showed an innocence he knew belied what was truly in her mind. "Is that all right with you?"

"Sure. We'll call it conserving water."

"Um, good idea." She stepped forward. "It's a good thing all those favorite places of yours deliver, because something tells me this shower just might sap all your energy," she crooned.

Pete drew in a sharp breath when her caresses grew more intimate and her mouth performed magic on his lips.

"Yeah, I think you're right. I'll probably need to lie down for awhile."

"YOU CALLED HIM AGAIN?" Pete found it difficult to sound irate when he was lying in bed naked except for the sheet draped across his hips, and holding a slice of mushroom pizza.

"I scared him spitless." Brianne was obviously proud of herself.

He closed his eyes and groaned. "Why did you call him again? He went after me today because he figured I was behind the first call."

"He didn't hurt you, did he?" She touched his cheek with her fingertips, relishing the roughness of his skin under her touch.

"Of course not! Still, your call last night did scare him pretty good. He kept saying I'd dreamed up this stunt, since I couldn't find any proof he'd killed you."

"And?" she pressed, sensing more. "What? What?" she insisted, crawling over to sit on his lap.

For a moment, Pete's thoughts were elsewhere, until Brianne threatened to twist his ear out of shape unless he told her.

"And one thing I noticed was that he was scared," he said simply.

She would have bounced up in glee if he hadn't caught her in time.

"Don't do any damage to the toys, sweetheart," he advised.

Brianne wrinkled her nose at his playful tone before telling him her share of the story. "Today I reminded him what happened before he killed me," she explained. "I told him things only I would have known."

"That was risky," he murmured.

"Not when he doesn't know I'm not who I was," Brianne argued. "Besides, it might shove him over the edge and he'll confess."

Pete shook his head. "I'm not sure that will be enough. But no more calls. At least wait a few days," he suggested. "You do too much and he'll get suspicious. I don't want him to lose it too soon."

Brianne settled back onto her side of the bed and leaned on the pillows propped up against the headboard. "I just want him punished."

"So do I. Look, I'll give Rick a call in the morning. I'll tell him about Whit going after me and suggest that they keep an eye on him. Okay?"

She agreed she'd settle for that. "As long as you call him first thing."

"No problem there. Whit isn't one of Rick's favorite people, either. I'll also tell him I've got a hunch Whit's dealing again, and he might want to let Narcotics know about it." He pulled another slice of pizza out of the box and offered it to her.

Brianne took the slice and bit down, chewing daintily. "Too bad Michael couldn't have come back as someone else and help us find his murderer," she mused. "I wonder if we could put an ad in the personals. 'Were you murdered by your fiancé? Are you in someone else's body now? Call us and we'll straighten it all out together.'"

He shook his head at her flight of whimsy. "And what if he tells you it was Brianne?"

She shook her head. "No, I've thought long and hard about it. If she had killed Michael, she would have to have had an excellent reason for doing so. Such as if he attacked her and she needed to defend herself. But I honestly don't feel that's how it happened."

"Self-defense doesn't hold when she had the gun right there," Pete interjected.

"Mathias said it was up to me," Brianne murmured, looping a string of cheese around her finger and sticking it in her mouth. "Which means it's up to me to find the killer. Naturally, he wouldn't give me any hints," she grumbled.

"What if I throw out names?" he suggested. "Sheila?"

She closed her eyes and cast about in her mind, but nothing happened. She slowly shook her head.

"No, it doesn't seem right. I can't see them having an affair. Oh, I know Michael liked to hit on pretty much every female he met, but Sheila loves Trey dearly, and adores her social status even more. She wouldn't do anything to jeopardize it. Besides, she and Trey were together that evening, which means he would be covering up for her, and I can't see him lying for her if she was having an affair."

"All right. Trey then."

Brianne tried the same mental exercise. "Same thing. He wouldn't want to do anything that would cast a bad light on the stores. And being accused of killing Michael would do that. Especially with Michael being a company executive."

"But you being accused wouldn't be as bad?" Pete asked wryly.

"Not when I don't hold as important a position and am basically expendable." Brianne reached for a napkin and wiped her fingers clean. She eyed another slice, considered she had been eating quite a lot lately, then shrugged her shoulders and took it. After all, she rationalized, she did need to keep up her strength.

"We could always consider the butler."

She shook her head. "That only happens in movies and books."

"That leaves one of the maids, your mother's nurse or your dear mother," Pete stated. "Think any of them could have done it?"

"Only one of the maids lives in. Mrs. Chambers, Mother's nurse, had that night off and was out of the house, and Mother..." She stopped. Whatever she'd been about to say had totally escaped her.

Pete noticed the odd look on her face. "What?"

Brianne tried again. She forced herself back to that night. Was there anyone else in the room with them? She sensed there had been. Things had been such a blur as she'd opened her eyes and found herself standing over Michael's body, the gun in her hand.

"No, I would surely have noticed the sound of her wheelchair," she murmured. "To be honest, I haven't thought much about that night. I had undergone so many shocks by then." She made a face. "After which I had to spend the night in a very disgusting jail cell. I don't care what they say, those places smell terrible!"

He put an arm around her shoulders and drew her against his side. "I wish I could have prevented all of that for you."

"You didn't know me then, remember?" she teased.

"I've got to admit you've handled all of this very well," Pete told her. "I can't think of anyone else who'd keep their sense of humor through it."

"I quickly understood I had no choice and that I'd better make the best of it. Mathias was a big help, too. Since no one else can hear him, he could prompt me through tricky situations, so I knew people's names and where I was supposed to go. I felt the worst when I realized I'd basically lost all of my friends," she confessed. "I already knew the last person I wanted to call was Lisa."

"The blond barracuda," Pete muttered.

Brianne narrowed her eyes. "Did she try anything with you?"

"I managed to escape with my virtue intact," he assured her.

She heaved a dramatic sigh. "And here I thought I'd have the pleasure of pulling out her hair by its artfully bleached roots."

"You might want to lay off any violence until after we settle this other case."

"True, but she's still on my list." Brianne inspected her nails. "I have to admit I like Brianne's body. She has great hair, nails that grow like crazy, and I've been able to truthfully shave a few years off my age. Not many women can do that."

"I knew I was crazy when I realized it didn't matter what you look like on the outside," he told her. "It was what's on the inside that really counts." Pete put the pizza box on the floor and turned back to Brianne. He lifted up the sheet and looked under it. "Still, the outside is a pretty nice package, and I guess it would have taken something this drastic for us to get together."

She held out her arms. "You know something, Hackett? I really should have accepted that dinner invitation years ago."

"Yeah, but I guess it's better late than never."

All laughter suddenly gone, Brianne studied his face, looking for something she felt was very important.

"This isn't going to end when the case is over, is it?" she asked softly. "We're not going to shake hands and part company like two civilized human beings, are we?"

Pete grew still. "Is that what you want?"

She knew she was taking a chance revealing her feelings, but she felt she had to know. "No. Do you?"

"Think Olivia would like having a P.I. around? Or do you think she'll start keeping rottweilers on the property to keep me off it?"

"Considering I told her today I'd be finding my own place, I don't think you'll need to worry about her," she said.

Pete was surprised at her revelation and guessed

correctly that the conversation hadn't gone well. "What did she say?"

Her insecurity surfaced. "She suggested I not rush into anything, since my future accommodations might be courtesy of the state."

Pete uttered a few choice descriptions of the woman. "Why would a mother even say such a thing?"

"Maybe she's jealous that she can't do as much as she used to," Brianne said idly. "I guess she was edged out when Trey took over the stores. Who knows? I think she's just a bitter woman who doesn't feel better unless she's insulting a member of her family. It's something she can't control, and she loves to be in control of everything."

Pete didn't agree, because he had a hunch there was more to it. He just had to find out what.

Chapter Fifteen

Brianne didn't want to wake up. Not when she was having such a wonderful dream, one that could have been out of a movie. She and Pete were lost in a canyon. Their clothes were in tatters and they were sunburned. But it didn't matter, because they were together, discomfort be damned.

She sighed softly and burrowed farther under the covers as she saw their clothing magically disappear. Amazing that what looked like hard ground could feel so soft.

Before the dream could turn more X-rated, she heard a whirring sound in the distance. "No, not the rescue helicopter already," she moaned, shaking her head in vehement denial.

"It's the phone," she heard Pete mumble. He leaned over her prone form and snagged the receiver.

"We don't have a phone," she muttered, slowly surfacing from her deep sleep. She could hear Pete's voice rumbling in the background, then a few curses as he leaned back over her to hang the phone up.

"Bri, wake up."

She protested, but he didn't stop shaking her shoulder. "You have to wake up," he insisted.

Something in his voice finally penetrated her sleep-induced fog. She opened her eyes and saw the tension on his face.

"What?" She sat up, pushing her hair away from her face. "What's wrong?" She started to fear the worst. "Is it about my case?"

"In a way." He took a deep breath. "Whit's in jail for attempted murder...and your death."

Brianne's eyes widened to saucer size. "What?"

"He got antsy last night and went looking to score, since his supplier didn't show up. Obviously, the drugs did a number on his mind when he ran into a brunette outside one of his favorite haunts. He started screaming that it was Allie and that he wasn't about to let her haunt him anymore. He went after her with a knife—probably the same one he used on you. The bouncer heard her screams and got outside just in time to wrestle the knife away from him. Luckily, she'd fought back and scratched Whit up pretty good. When the cops showed up, he was still going on about how she was Allie Walker come back to haunt him. They figured it for drug-induced psychosis and took him down to the psych ward. Rick was in there talking to him early this morning. Whit was a lot more coherent then and told him every detail of your death. He said he knew if he didn't tell someone you'd continue to haunt him. Rick feels it's a pretty strong case even if Whit's attorney is trying to claim the drugs were behind his confession and his claims of you haunting him."

Brianne screamed in glee, throwing her arms around him. "It worked! It worked!"

"There's still a fine line," he warned her.

She shook her head. "No, Mathias said it would all work out and he was right!" She bounced up and down in her excitement. "If Whit can be brought to justice, there's no reason why Michael's murderer can't be, too."

"It's nothing more than coincidence," Pete argued.

"No, it's righting a wrong," she corrected. "Do you know something? Me, with barely a high-school education, worked up a new marketing plan for the stores. And most of the department managers liked it! I'm going to bring Sinclairs into the nineties!" Her face glowed with excitement. "I never thought I'd have a chance like this to show what I can do. But they're listening to me."

"I'm glad, honey, really glad for you," he said sincerely, even as he wondered if the time wouldn't come when she'd realized she'd outgrown him. After all, what would a fancy socialite want with a crusty P.I. like him?

"There's no guarantee this will work out." She'd read his mind. "And for all I know, when this is all over, I could be back to waiting tables again."

"Would that bother you?"

Brianne looped her arms around his neck. "Only if you're not there."

"People will say I'm after your money," he warned. "And your mother will be at the head of the pack."

"And some of them will say I'm after your body," she teased. "Something tells me I'm getting the better part of the deal." She puckered up for a playful kiss.

He leaned over to kiss her, then paused. "We won't have to live with Olivia, will we?"

Brianne dared not think about weddings and what comes afterward. This was still all too new. The idea of their living together was only in the planning stage. Plus she had to contend with a murder charge hanging over her head.

"Just give me a chance to jazz up this place."

Pete was surprised and touched by her comment. He didn't exactly live in the best neighborhood. "It's not a place you'd invite your friends to."

"Considering the friends the old Brianne had, I won't miss them." She bounced out of bed and stopped to pull on one of Pete's T-shirts. "You're in luck. When I bought the beer last night, I also picked up breakfast makings."

He widened his eyes mockingly. "She cooks, too!"

"Be careful or you'll find cayenne pepper in your eggs."

It wasn't until Brianne left the room that Pete realized, during all the talk about her mother, he hadn't mentioned he was seeing Trey and Olivia that day.

As he climbed out of bed and pulled clean clothing out of the chest of drawers, he started to think about the upcoming interviews. Maybe, in a sense, what had worked for Whit just might bring out some necessary truth among the Sinclair family.

PETE WASN'T LONG into his talk with Trey before he realized the man truly believed his sister had killed her fiancé. But that Trey didn't blame her for it.

"I'm actually glad I wasn't there to see anything concrete," he confessed to Pete. "They had been having problems for some time, and obviously, that night it all came out."

"Because Matthews was fooling around," Pete stated, staring at his cassette machine and silently damning the information he was recording.

Trey nodded. "But I don't think she meant to shoot him, much less kill him. She probably just wanted to scare him."

"Mr. Sinclair, you didn't say any of this to the police, did you?" Pete asked.

"Of course not! If they want to prosecute Bri, they'll have to come up with more than the nonsense they've been spouting." He drew himself up to his full height. "Brianne isn't unstable." He lowered his voice. "That was Mother's idea. She didn't know what else would work. I just wish Brianne could remember that night, so we'd all know how it happened."

Pete snapped off the recorder. "What if Brianne did remember the truth about that night?" he said casually.

Trey leaned forward, looking more interested than worried. "Has she? Would that hurt her case or help it? It's bad enough that she's been acting so strange lately—coming up with outlandish ideas for the store, buying all those colorful clothes." He shook his head. "It's not like her. But I think she would feel better if she remembered what had happened."

If you only knew, Pete thought.

"I know the two of you are seeing each other," Trey said slowly.

"I guess that makes your mother real happy," he drawled.

Trey grimaced. "Mother can be difficult at times," he said with admirable understatement.

Pete's silent agreement was more profane.

Trey looked a little uncomfortable. "I just want to say that if Brianne's happy, that's all that counts. I know it seems odd, what with Michael so recently..." His voice dropped off. "But what they had wasn't real. That's why I won't protest whatever you two decide. I saw her face when she looked at you that night you came here. And she looked happy."

"Are you saying you're giving us your seal of approval?"

He nodded. "Actually, anyone who can stand up to Mother the way you did that night needs to be around more."

For a brief moment, the two men shared common ground.

"Trey, shouldn't you be on your way?"

It wasn't until Olivia's voice intruded that Pete realized she had arrived with no sound at all. He was surprised her motorized wheelchair was so quiet as she moved farther into the carpeted room.

As always, she was dressed conservatively—not one hair out of place, pearls at her throat and ears. She stared at Trey, who immediately mumbled he had to be leaving and fled from the room.

"Why don't we begin, since I'm sure your time is valuable, Mr. Hackett," she said in her imperious tone. "After all, my daughter is paying for you." A tiny smile appeared at the edge of her lips as she noted the tightening of his. Direct hit.

"Fine." He reached into his briefcase and pulled out a blank cassette, which he inserted in the recorder. "I hope you don't mind if I tape our conversation."

She inclined her head. "Not at all. That way we both know you'll have all the facts set down correctly."

Pete pulled out a notebook and opened it, consulting the contents.

"I'm still puzzled about one thing. Why do you honestly feel Brianne is no longer your daughter?" He looked up, schooling his expression to reflect nothing more than curiosity.

Olivia showed no reaction to his question. "All I have to do is look at her and know that she is not the daughter I bore," she said slowly and distinctly. "My daughter would not have dreamed of acting in the manner this woman has. She would not have allowed someone to style her hair in such an unsuitable way and she wouldn't wear such colorful clothing. She also wouldn't argue with me so enthusiastically. Brianne has always been a lovely and quiet woman. This person is not."

He nodded, as if she made perfect sense. He had to admit he was awed by her impression of the new Brianne.

"So what do you think happened to *your* Brianne?"

"I have no idea. Shouldn't we be talking about her case?"

"It's not all that easy when you believe she isn't your daughter," he replied. "You know, the shock of Mr. Matthews's death affected Brianne in many ways. Such as how she behaves. She feels after seeing death, she wants to embrace life."

"Then she should have found a more appropriate way of embracing it."

"It also has to do with her memory of that night coming back."

If he'd hoped for a reaction, he was sorely disappointed. "Now you know why our attorney suggested diminished capacity," the woman said with a sniff. "Her memory of that night is severely impaired."

"Not exactly." He turned a leaf in his notebook. With the way he had it angled, Olivia had no way of knowing he was staring at blank pages. "She knew she wasn't alone in the room."

A faint flicker in her eyes told him he was on the right track.

"I will not allow you to accuse Trey of anything just because you hope to see her set free," she said coldly.

"I wasn't thinking about Trey, Mrs. Sinclair," he said in a reasonable tone. "I was thinking of someone who could enter a room without anyone knowing it. Someone who knew where Brianne kept her gun—a weapon that your alleged "new" Brianne would know nothing about. Someone who might have a reason to want Matthews dead."

"Now, why would I want him dead?" Olivia asked in the same tone she might use to request tea.

Now Pete knew he was on the right track. All those instincts from working homicide had come back with a vengeance and told him he was going to get exactly what he was after: the truth. But he had to press and press hard, because that was the only thing this woman would understand.

"That's funny, I don't recall saying you in particular. Still, there could be a variety of reasons why you'd decide the world was better off without him. Maybe you felt he was bringing the wrong kind of attention to your family name. A name, understand, that you've diligently protected since the day of your marriage. You figured if he could be unfaithful during his engagement, he would continue to be during the marriage. And while adultery isn't the major scandal it used to be, it would be a major one in your eyes. I don't know. Maybe, you came downstairs and overheard Brianne tell him she was breaking off their engagement. Maybe Matthews was pouring on the charm, telling her he loved her and he'd do anything to keep her. And maybe she was weakening."

He leaned forward, deliberately invading her space. He had to give her a lot of credit, for she didn't blink an eye. "Except you knew he was lying. Not to mention you really didn't like him, even if you gave that impression to the public. One thing you forgot. There're people out there who sensed he wasn't your idea of the perfect fiancé and were willing to say so. It looked like Trey was the only one who liked him, and that was because he didn't see the man's flaws. But you saw them from the beginning. It didn't matter when he merely worked for you. After all, you could always arrange to have him fired, right? But things changed when he romanced Brianne and asked her to marry him. That night, you probably didn't even think about it. You went back upstairs, got Brianne's gun, came back and shot him. Brianne probably couldn't handle the idea of her mother shooting her fiancé, so she went into shock and wiped out the memory. Because she was in shock, you had no problem pressing the gun into her hand and letting her think she killed him," he said with deceptive softness. "No wonder she wanted nothing to do with you after that. She saw you shoot a man she might have loved, and while after the fact she might not have remembered it happening, something inside her told her your hands were dirty. She couldn't handle it."

Olivia still hadn't reacted to anything he said, but Pete would have bet his Porsche he was right on the money.

"If she loved him so much, why did she jump into your bed so readily?"

"Because with me, she found out what real love is," Pete replied, not at all insulted by her tone. "Maybe you should have waited, Olivia." He deliberately used her first name. "I don't think Brianne would have allowed Matthews to talk her into taking back his ring." He flexed his fingers at his sides. It was taking a lot of effort not to clench them into fists. "What I can't understand is why you would allow your own daughter to think she committed a murder. Why you would have sat back and let her go to trial and probably be convicted because of the evidence against her." Contempt colored his voice. "Funny, I always thought mothers protected their daughters, instead of throwing them to the wolves."

Olivia's tiny smile didn't waver. "She was a weak link. Trey lived for the business, and he saw things my way. Brianne didn't. Plus she made the mistake of falling in love with the wrong man. She had to pay for it. What does it matter who pulled the trigger? The man is out of the way. You should be happy about that. Oh, I'm certain Brianne will be incarcerated for some time, but when you think of her trust fund, I'm sure you'll be more than willing to wait for her."

Pete hadn't thought he would ever want to hit a woman. But then he hadn't met a cold bitch like Olivia before. It was difficult to keep his fury hidden, but he knew Brianne's future hinged on it.

"Money and social position isn't the be-all and end-all for everyone," he argued. "You also forget her memory might come back and she'll tell everything."

"I don't think anyone would believe her after this late date. No, she'll have to pay." The dowager settled back in her wheelchair. "She really should have accepted Joshua's advice, and it would have been all over by now. I will hate the adverse publicity a trial brings, but I guess it can't be helped. She needn't worry. Her family will stand behind her. It's the least we can do."

"You did it, didn't you? You shot Michael!"

Olivia's face turned paper white as she turned to see her son storming into the room.

Trey didn't stop until he loomed over her. "Everything Pete said is true, isn't it? You shot Michael because your twisted mind couldn't handle the fact that Brianne might have married him, after all. Now I remember how you used to bring up little snippets of gossip about him and his secretary, or someone else, just to hurt her. You didn't care how much you did hurt her as long as she didn't marry him. But to go so far as to kill him?" His face contorted with the horror he obviously felt.

"It was for the good of the family!" she snapped.

That was enough for Pete. He quietly got up and walked over to the nearest phone. Seconds later he was talking to Rick. In the background he could hear Olivia trying to convince her distraught son that she had a good reason for what she had done. Except he wasn't having any of it.

"Get over to the Sinclair house fast," Pete advised his ex-partner.

"What've you got?"

He exhaled the breath he felt he had been holding for years. "The truth."

"MATHIAS SAID her daughter couldn't handle it. It's no wonder why," Brianne murmured after Pete filled her in about the day's events. They'd just watched footage of Olivia being taken to police headquarters on the evening news.

The moment Rick showed up, Pete had told him what had happened and explained that Trey had also called an attorney. Luckily, Trey had no intention of lying for his mother. Olivia had tried to convince him that it was better off if Brianne continued to be the accused, but he was having none of it. He loved his mother and told her so, but he wouldn't allow an innocent person to go to prison just because Olivia felt her daughter should pay for choosing the wrong man.

Pete felt wiped out. As soon as he got back to his office, he'd called Rhyder and told him what had happened, and the lawyer had assured him he'd handle the paperwork necessary to clear Brianne of any charges. Afterward, Pete had called Brianne. He didn't tell her what her mother had said, merely that the interview had been more than he'd hoped for. They'd made plans to meet at his apartment at the end of the day, with Brianne promising to bring dinner.

The barbecued ribs she brought were messy but excellent. Pete hadn't thought he had an appetite until he inhaled the spicy sauce.

"How could she have hated me that much?" Brianne looked pensive for a moment. "There has to be a lot more to it than just her considering Michael the wrong man."

"If so, I don't think you'll ever find out. I wouldn't worry about her. She'll probably cop an insanity plea and spend the time in a quiet room that was originally meant for you." He was derisive on that point. He hadn't wanted to see Brianne there and he didn't want to see Olivia there for an entirely different reason. He knew she was aware of what she was doing all the time. But a frail-looking woman in a wheelchair, even if she had a backbone of tempered steel, wouldn't make a likely candidate for the state prison. Even if she deserved it.

He wiped his hands with moistened towelettes provided with the ribs and ensnared Brianne in his grasp.

"Think you could spruce this place up so you wouldn't mind living here?" he asked casually.

"No problem there." She was trying to act as casually as he was.

"You know we both have adjustments to make."

She turned her head so she could better see him. "I don't mind, if you don't."

My dear, for once be frank with the man! Admittedly, it isn't a marriage proposal, but perhaps the two of you should wait for that, anyway.

"Mathias?" She was so stunned at hearing his voice that she spoke his name out loud.

Pete stiffened. "He's talking to you?"

She nodded.

Tell Peter not to worry about my popping in at odd times. You've accomplished what you've needed to, Brianne. You've made sure Allie's murderer would pay for his crime, and Michael's murderer will do the same. You have the kind of employment that will utilize your hidden talents and you have a man who loves you. I suggest you make sure not to do anything to ruin it.

"Is this goodbye?" she asked, feeling a sense of loss. He'd been a part of her for so long.

You don't need me anymore, Brianne. You'll do fine on your own. I know you will. Goodbye, my dear. I must say you've livened up my existence.

Brianne wasn't sure how, but she knew he was gone.

"He told me goodbye," she said in a small voice. "He told me I did what I needed to do, that I have a job that's perfect for me and I'll do fine."

"Is that all he said?"

She turned around fully in his arms and slid hers around his waist. "He also said something about a man." She cocked her head to one side. "Let's see, you're a man."

"I'm glad to see you figured that out."

"And I'm a woman." She began unbuttoning his shirt. "And what with the way things worked out, we must be meant for each other."

"Tell me something I don't already know." He was busy pulling her cobalt blue blouse out of her matching pants. He was surprised to see her lingerie matched the clothing. "You know, princess, something tells me you're going to keep me surprised for a long time."

She was already busy nibbling at his lips. "The something telling you that is fate," she whispered against his parted lips. "Fate brought us together and fate means to make sure we stay together."

"Always did like a woman who knew her own mind."

Brianne smiled. "Good, because something tells me this is just the beginning for us."

Weddings by DeWilde

Since the turn of the century the elegant and
fashionable DeWilde stores have helped brides
around the world turn the fantasy of their
"Special Day" into reality. But now the store
and three generations of family are torn apart
by the divorce of Grace and Jeffrey DeWilde.
As family members face new challenges and
loves—and a long-secret mystery—the lives of
Grace and Jeffrey intermingle with store
employees, friends and relatives in this fast-
paced, glamorous, internationally set series. For
weddings and romance, glamour and fun-filled
entertainment, enter the world of DeWilde...

Twelve remarkable books, coming to you
once a month, beginning in April 1996

Weddings by DeWilde begins with
Shattered Vows
by Jasmine Cresswell

Here's a preview!

"SPEND THE NIGHT with me, Lianne."

No softening lies, no beguiling promises, just the curt offer of a night of sex. She closed her eyes, shutting out temptation. She had never expected to feel this sort of relentless drive for sexual fulfillment, so she had no mechanisms in place for coping with it. "No." The one-word denial was all she could manage to articulate.

His grip on her arms tightened as if he might refuse to accept her answer. Shockingly, she wished for a split second that he would ignore her rejection and simply bundle her into the car and drive her straight to his flat, refusing to take no for an answer. All the pleasures of mindless sex, with none of the responsibility. For a couple of seconds he neither moved nor spoke. Then he released her, turning abruptly to open the door on the passenger side of his Jaguar. "I'll drive you home," he said, his voice hard and flat. "Get in."

The traffic was heavy, and the rain started again as an annoying drizzle that distorted depth perception made driving difficult, but Lianne didn't fool herself that the silence inside the car was caused by the driving conditions. The air around them crackled and sparked with their thwarted desire. Her body was still on fire. Why didn't Gabe say something? she thought, feeling aggrieved.

Perhaps because he was finding it as difficult as she was to think of something appropriate to say. He was thirty years old, long past the stage of needing to bed a woman just so he could record another sexual conquest in his little black book. He'd spent five months dating Julia, which suggested he was a man who valued friendship as an element in his relationships with women. Since he didn't seem to like her very much, he was probably as embarrassed as she was by the stupid, inexplicable intensity of their physical response to each other.

"Maybe we should just set aside a weekend to have wild, uninterrupted sex," she said, thinking aloud. "Maybe that way we'd get whatever it is we feel for each other out of our systems and be able to move on with the rest of our lives."

His mouth quirked into a rueful smile. "Isn't that supposed to be my line?"

"Why? Because you're the man? Are you sexist enough to believe that women don't have sexual urges? I'm just as aware of what's going on between us as you are, Gabe. Am I supposed to pretend I haven't noticed that we practically ignite whenever we touch? And that we have nothing much in common except mutual lust—and a good friend we betrayed?"

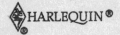

What do women really want to know?

Trust the world's largest publisher of
women's fiction to tell you.

HARLEQUIN ULTIMATE GUIDES™

I CAN FIX THAT

A Guide For Women
Who Want To Do It Themselves

This is the only guide a self-reliant
woman will ever need to deal
with those pesky items that
break, wear out or just don't work
anymore. Chock-full of friendly
advice and straightforward,
step-by-step solutions to the
trials of everyday life in our
gadget-oriented world! So, don't
just sit there wondering how to
fix the VCR—run to your
nearest bookstore for your copy now!

Available this May, at your favorite retail outlet.

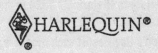

HARLEQUIN®

The Magic Wedding Dress

Imagine a wedding dress that costs a million dollars.
Imagine a wedding dress that allows the wearer to
find her one true love—not always the man she
thinks it is. And then imagine a wedding dress that
brings out all the best attributes in its bride, so that
every man who glimpses her is sure to fall in love.
Karen Toller Whittenburg imagined just such a dress
and allowed it to take on a life of its own in her new
American Romance trilogy, *The Magic Wedding Dress*.
Be sure to catch all three:

March
#621—THE MILLION-DOLLAR BRIDE

May
#630—THE FIFTY-CENT GROOM

August
#643—THE TWO-PENNY WEDDING

Come along and dream with Karen Toller
Whittenburg!

WDRESS1

AMERICAN ❖ ROMANCE®

With only forty-eight hours to lasso their mates—
it's a stampede...to the altar!

WILD WEST
Weddings

by Cathy Gillen Thacker

Looking down from above, Montana maven
Max McKendrick wants to make sure his heirs get
something money can't buy—true love! And if his two
nephews and niece want to inherit their piece of his
sprawling Silver Spur ranch then they'll have to wed the
spouse of *his* choice—within forty-eight hours!

Don't miss any of the Wild West Weddings titles!

#625 THE COWBOY'S BRIDE (April)

#629 THE RANCH STUD (May)

#633 THE MAVERICK MARRIAGE (June)

WWW

HARLEQUIN
AMERICAN ◆ ROMANCE ®

Once in a while, there's a story so special, a story so unusual,
that your pulse races, your blood rushes. We call this

AMERICAN
ROMANCE
heart beat

LOVER'S LEAP is one such story.

As if pushed, a near-naked man jumped into Maggie Macintyre's canoe, toppling
them into the churning river. But her anger at the wild man with the long raven
hair and the hard bronze body disappeared when she saw the intensity of a lover's
longing in the depths of his black eyes...as if he'd loved her for a century or
more. But who was this stranger who'd told her she was the woman of his dreams?

#632 LOVER'S LEAP
by
Pamela Browning
May 1996

HEART12

Fall in love all over again with

This Time... MARRIAGE

In this collection of original short stories, three brides get a unique chance for a return engagement!

- Being kidnapped from your bridal shower by a one-time love can really put a crimp in your wedding plans! *The Borrowed Bride*— by **Susan Wiggs**, *Romantic Times* Career Achievement Award-winning author.

- After fifteen years a couple reunites for the sake of their child—this time will it end in marriage? *The Forgotten Bride*—by **Janice Kaiser**.

- It's tough to make a good divorce stick—especially when you're thrown together with your ex in a magazine wedding shoot! *The Bygone Bride*— by **Muriel Jensen**.

Don't miss THIS TIME...MARRIAGE, available in April wherever Harlequin books are sold.

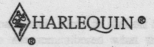

HARLEQUIN ®